ORION'S WEB

ALEXANDRA MANFIELD

Spindle
PRESS

First published by Spindle Press, 2022

Title: Orion's Web/Alexandra Manfield, author.

ISBN: 9780648686798

Cover Design: Shkike/99designs

1

ANNA

$\mathcal{I}$ am Anna Drake. On the day I was born, the fires went out and the women talked of thunder. Their walk to shelter brought me on a week before my time. My mother says an early child is a lucky child because she carries a few spare days to use at the end of her life.

I really hope that's true.

Tonight, I am waiting and tiring of waiting. I stare into the dark. The fire behind me cracks and hisses. Gardner is coming; Freya is sure. She closes her eyes, yawns, and nestles in to sleep. I smooth a strand of hair from her face, feel a little huff of breath: her last fight for the day, and then the uneven rhythm of her dreaming sleep. Brave Freya, so sure in my arms.

I ache from holding her and try to shift my weight. The ground is hard and cold, my muscles locked in place. I look into the night, trying to part the rolling waves of darkness to see the glow of his fire. *Hurry, Gardner.*

There—the soft scuff of heels. Finally. I look up to see his fire moving up and down, leaving orange comet trails against the black. Gardner steps into the glow, his firestick flaring against the tinkle of red coals. He drives the stick into the sand so that it illuminates a circle around us, throws down a thick blanket and squats to unfold it. Then he lifts Freya from me and gently settles her onto the blanket. I tuck the corners around her. A musty animal smell emanates from it.

"A horse? Out here?"

He shrugs. "Lucky for us."

I roll the last log onto the fire, recoiling from the sparks as the coals collapse beneath it. Gardner steps up beside me, warms one hand against the flames, and pulls an apple from his pocket. The sight of this round, green thing, incongruous in the desert night, evokes a deep yearning within me for pink and white blossoms, for its tart crispness, and for my mother, shining up a newly picked Sundowner on her shirt for me. I'm not even sure if this is memory or a species of collective nostalgia; a cellular response to apple-deprivation. Gardner plants it gently in my hands and I savour the feel of it in my palms.

We settle in front of the fire. He lies on the sand and is soon snoring softly. Sitting cross-legged near Freya, I eat my apple and stare out beyond the flame into a night of stars.

When he awakes to take his turn on watch, I don't fall immediately into dreaming, instead I lie against Freya's warmth, remembering, searching through the spinning fog of time to find a moment I would change...

I REMEMBER WALLABY-GRAZED GRASS, soft beneath my feet.

It was a short walk during the day, but now, under the

moon's bright gaze, the lawn stretches like a yawn towards the forest.

I run, and the cold, clear night catches at my heels. I dive beneath the canopy, stumbling and tripping over ferns and logs until I find a rough trunk to lean against and catch my breath. As my heart quietens, I hear a shift of bark, a fallen twig; a night creature above me.

"Shama?"

Not yet.

And then I think I hear whale-song. I am surely under water, and the trees are kelp reaching up towards the surface of the sea. But it is not a whale. It is Shama. Her singing stops, and she lands in front of me with a soundless leap. The moon casts a shadow tracery of twigs and branches on her skin. Her hair is a wild tangle, studded with leaves and burrs. Finger to lips, she signals silence, as though my simple act of breathing is too loud. Then she turns and leaps into the underbrush. A half glance backwards. *Follow me.*

A willie wagtail calls from the edge of the meadow behind us; his song, a promise to protect his young and their home, even in the moon's revealing light. Shama has told me many secrets, and they have soaked into my bones. She doesn't speak of the nesting bird tonight though, as she leads us through the forest.

We move deeper in. A chill settles around my shoulders, my ears, and cheeks. Shama leads me through a tangle of pomaderris and daisy-bush to the cold, ringing call of the river. The moss begins where the eucalypts succumb to ancient myrtle beeches; gnarled old ones, holding Gondwana in their hearts. Shama is quick, full of urgency, and I am falling behind.

We reach easier walking under the canopy of the rainforest. Mud, carpeted with soft leaves, gives way beneath my feet. I follow her ghost-limbed leaps between the trees until we reach a wide beach of rough sand at the river's edge. Small lights flicker in mossy crevices and reflect from the glistening surfaces of wet boulders. Shama sits cross-legged on the sand and I find a rock to perch on.

"Shama?" She doesn't turn her head. I take a deep breath; the nutmeg scent of sassafras fizzles through my lungs and into my blood; my cheeks flare with warmth and I wait.

A scented breeze funnels towards me, parting the cold waves of night air. Above the river, a glow appears.

The river stops its running.

All sound ceases.

The light grows and spreads, turns from blue to yellow to white until it mushrooms like a bomb, blinding me.

When my eyes adjust, I see Shama; a statue, open-eyed. The moon has come to rest upon the river, its borrowed light pulsing through the time-frozen forest. I cannot comprehend its brightness. My heart can't contain it, nor my mind explain it. The orb moves—pulsating, stretching and returning; something of many faces. Or perhaps I see many faces within it, finding fragments of meaning on that which is so much more. Then the orb expands. Its edge touches me and I feel warmth against my skin. The warmth enters me, nourishing as it moves within, rippling through me as though I am only water. And I am. And it is enough.

With a ringing of bright bells, the light vanishes and the roar of the water returns. Shama jumps up and turns towards me, her face alight. I'm at once full and empty; full of its light and warmth, and yet forever bereft.

"The Heart of the World," she says, taking my hands. "Take it. Keep it safe for us for the times that are to come."

SHAMA...

Her name recedes into a whisper and I awaken. The night's cold has seeped into my body; my hip aches from the hard ground and I dare not move my arm deadened by Freya's sleeping weight, for fear I might wake her. Yet I'm grateful; I have slept for the first time in many nights, the earth beneath me less a sleep-thwarting demon and more a solid friend.

Gardner has gone again. He'll return with meat. My mouth is dry. When Freya wakes, I'll drink. I look up through the sparse, swaying leaves above us to a sky blue with morning. The sun on my cheeks already has warmth in it. Freya makes a small sound and twitches in her last dream.

My daughter is not like other children. On the night she was born, the Southern Lights could be seen as far north as the mainland. An hour after the last pink strains of sunset had left the sky, and heavy with the swells of labour, I walked out under the clear night—pacing and rocking. The cold light of Venus stood in for the moon and I was mesmerised by the velvet pitch of the sky. Green ghost lights flickered tentative fingers, built into rolling sheets of glowing light; yellow, green and blue, passing across the arch of the heavens in hypnotic waves that pulled my body into synchrony with their undulating ions. For hours I was held by the great hands of the aurora. With each wave the rending pain would build until it was almost too much to bear, only to dissipate, another mere flicker of colour, into the vast night sky.

I was not alone after that. Not really. The moon rose; a half boat, enough light to see by. And finally, in a dance and push beneath the stars, my body opened like a chasm and Freya was expelled from me. She was slippery and hot and heavy in my arms as I caught her. We shivered together. She lay against me; suckling, watching. Her eyes were grey and bright in the moonlight. Her face, once I'd wiped it clear of the smear of birth, glowed with more than the moon's white glare, as though the heart of the world shone from within her.

I watch her eyelids flutter open now; her eyes are a lucid brown in this morning light and I kiss her sleep-reddened cheek.

"Good morning Mummy."

"Morning love."

"Where's Daddy?"

"Gone to find us some food. Here—have a drink." I pass her the water bottle; she drinks in big gulps, dribbling some down her front. I don't berate her for the waste. We'll find more soon; Gardner has a good nose for water.

I'm folding up the saddle-rug when I hear it. Freya is trailing a long stick around and around a tree. The sound begins as a low hum above the tick-a-tick-a-tick of her stick and grows louder, into a dark, thrumming roar.

"Freya!" She is standing wide-eyed and frozen. I drop the rug, run to her, grab her and fling her around behind the tree, holding her to me. The noise builds. She presses her hands against her ears and squeezes her eyes closed. After a few moments, the roar dies away. I hug her close.

"It's all right. It's gone."

We are still huddled beneath the tree when Gardner returns. He drops the rabbit and bounds up to us, pacing, circling us with worry. I reach out and grab at him.

"Gardner, stop!"

My hand clutches a solid wad of fur and he heaves his weight against us. Freya pops out from beneath my arm and launches herself at him. He drops to the ground and nuzzles her neck until she giggles.

I watch them, and for a moment we are free. At this distance I can taste it again—the wonder of it, the impossible strangeness of it: my daughter and the dingo, rolling in the sand.

Gardner is not like other men. He tells me he's not alone, that there are others like him; or that there were. But I have never met them.

WE WALK IN A LINE. It seems to end up that way, no matter how we start out. Gardner before us, nose to ground, tail a curious flag, and Freya just ahead of me, her small stride length warring with her eagerness to catch up to him. We've been travelling for over an hour since we started out this morning. She'll only go another few minutes more, I think, before she will stop and ask to be carried. I carry her mostly, though sometimes she'll get a bumpy ride on Gardner. She's getting stronger, more used to the routine, and she asks less and less about food. I just hope my waning milk supply will last.

I remind myself to look up every now and then from my feet and the orange sand. It's so easy not to, especially as the day wears on and the sun's gaze grows stronger. There is very little topography here, barely a hill or swathe to break the monotony. It is the land as we have always known it, but not the land our grandparents knew. Our father's fathers were warned, so amply, with such force and clarity, but though they watched the dial of the clock move surely towards the hour of twelve, they could not see its motion. Only when the hour was late did they concede that, despite the evidence of their senses, the final gong would strike. It has been ever thus—our common sense confounds us; because it is not common, or sense at all.

And so, we have returned to the climate of the Jurassic: acid seas and land laid desert-bare. I remember coolness and moisture, and mist and trees that swept the roof of the sky. And I remember Shama. Those places are but white standing ghost forests now, all bare wood that knocks like bones in the baking northerly breeze. No place for Shama, or for the creatures and the green that were in her care.

The red sands of the centre reach their fingers outwards and encroach ever further upon the ocean. We do not swim there much now—the jellyfish make it unpleasant and the acid water irritates our skin if we linger too long in its yellow embrace. We have been retreating from its once beloved shores for decades now; the tide rises higher every year and the sea is no longer itself.

My mother is an Outdweller. I lived with her until I was twelve and it was time for me to go to school. Then my father brought me to the Dome. I enjoyed it at first—the lights, the clothes, the food—all so rich and bright. We used our fabrics, our skin, to connect to the world and to each other. In the Dome, the strange blue of the day would fade to a pink-grey shroud at sundown; sunset muted by a barrier of solar cells. These cells lost their pigmentation at night but retained an opacity that dimmed the brightness of the stars— a fair compromise perhaps, for keeping the Dome's citizens within the perfect temperature range and supplying all their power needs. For me, I missed the brilliance and blackness of the sky at night.

My father sent me to boarding school, one of the very last beyond the edge of the Dome within the habitable zone. Bushfire was always a risk, but there were structures in place for that. It was thought to be education of the character for the wealthier city-dwellers to send their children to these most sought-after of locations; to be the privileged few to experience what humanity had once known as a birthright.

Our school was in the alpine region, established in one of the last true-climate towns in the State, after the habitable zone mapping had shown it to be a suitable refuge for the next fifty years. Forest surrounded us—tall, wet, mountain forest. We learnt that snow gum woodlands had once grown at the site our school now occupied. I would try to imagine them. *Snow gums.* The name, so exotic, so evocative. Of course, we all knew what snow was; still celebrated with the fake stuff each Christmas. But I had never seen any; not even a patch. I looked at pictures of these trees; their bark sinuous, green and silver, like shining skin, and I wondered at their dancing suppleness, even in their stillness, and at the light that spangled from leaves hung with ice.

The months after school, after Shama, were the loneliest. I returned to my father to live in his pod within the Dome. But a sky that never truly darkened; rain that fell on command—these were not for me. My father worked a lot, earned a lot. We saw little of each other. And when the day came that I told him I must return Outside, he didn't try to stop me, not really. I don't know if he'd grown weary of me, as one tires of a shiny new toy, or whether he came to realise that we did not share enough to fill the less than half an hour a day we spent in each other's company. He was growing older and perhaps his Outland adventuring, his romance with my mother and her people, seemed the mere follies of youth. I'm not sure he really knew where to put me; where I sat in his most rich and orderly life. So, I left the Dome, left my father, wondering only a little if he would miss me.

Now, as we trudge beneath a relentless blue sky, looking

down to shield our eyes from the glare, I wonder if we are doing the right thing by returning.

"Mummy?"

"Yes, love?"

"Where do bilbies go in the day?"

"They sleep in their cool burrows underground."

"Under the ground?"

"Yes."

It has been like this the last few weeks—question upon question, her mind searching to understand, to link, to know. I wonder if it helps her to gain some control over her ever-changing world, or whether it's just a normal part of being four. I wouldn't know; she's my only child. I don't really remember being her age. I imagine my mother would have answered all my questions with the patience of a desert stone, but I don't seem to share my mother's calm wisdom. I weary of conversation with my little one and hope she doesn't notice.

"Mummy?"

"Yes?"

"Do they live like Grandma?"

"Well…yes, yes they do. They live where they can feel safe from the brightness of the sun."

"Why is the sun so bright?"

I have always promised myself to speak truth to her, or as much of it as I can muster. But today I don't, not fully. I don't have the heart.

"It is like you my darling, it cannot help its radiance."

"What's radiance?"

Gardner nuzzles her armpit. She lifts her arm and squeals.

"Daddy!"

He seems to smile, but I look into his eyes—more than

canine, less than human—and see that we must hurry. He squats and she climbs onto his back.

We walk faster now. Freya leans her cheek against him, lulled by his even strides, and closes her eyes. The sky darkens. Leaden clouds scud in, gathering at an alarming rate. We must find shelter soon. It hasn't rained for weeks. We travelled in winter to avoid the relentless power of the sun; but in this season, when the heavens let loose, it is an intense downpour. Nothing is gentle these days.

We are both running by the time the first drops fall. Gardner has led us to a rocky hillock, the first of many we see in the long stretch towards the horizon ahead of us. Freya has fallen asleep. We scramble up, squeeze under an overhanging boulder, and I gather her into my arms. She doesn't awaken. I envy her trust, her complete sense of safety, while my skin prickles with fear as thunder booms all around us.

I can smell the heat off the rocks as it hisses into steam from the first sheet of rain. The water drips and pools just in front of us, and I'm thankful it's draining away, down the rock face, and not into our shelter. I rest against Gardner's warm bulk. He sits, front paws together, watching the downpour. I'm used to the silence of his company, but wish, not for the first time, that we could talk to relieve the tension building within me. He tells me he understands when I speak to him, but that the words are filtered through his canine perceptions and don't mean quite the same to him as they do when we speak at night, when he is a man.

I did not know him on that night I tripped and stumbled my way through the forest towards the open lawn that led back to my school, the glow of the unknowable light stretching my heart to breaking, the feel of Shama's last embrace still warm against my skin. She'd told me I would find him, but I hadn't understood her. Had not understood so much; why she chose me; why she had to leave; where she would go.

My last exam done; the line of black cars waited to take us home, back to the Dome, back to the bright, good city, where we could tell of our schooling experience to our parents, our clients, our children; use the illustrious name of the school, the knowing that comes from living as we once lived, to be peers in our world, leaders and builders. But I couldn't feel it as I left the vaulted halls and walked towards my father's waiting car. I yearned only for my mother, to return to her and other Outdwellers, to live the secrets that Shama had revealed to me, to tell her story, the story of the world that once was...

The rain eases as quickly as it has begun, leaving a temporary sea in its wake. I draw out a water bottle and place it below the dripping rock face until it's overflowing; this at least, is one boon of the downpour. We'll have to wait until some of the water has soaked into the desert earth before we can walk again. I fish inside my satchel for some dried meat, give some to Gardner and chew on another salty strip myself, being careful to leave a little for Freya. I move a long tangle of her brown hair away from her face and stroke her forehead. We should wake her soon or she won't settle well at night.

Gardner pricks his ears and raises himself off his haunches. I hear the thrum and rattle from far off. It grows steadily louder, heading our way. I place my hands lightly over Freya's ears, hoping she won't stir. This is the third time in as many days that we've encountered the ancient vehicle, but it only now occurs to me to wonder whether this is a coincidence. We watch the old fossil-fuel-powered 4WD splash through the puddles just below our sheltering place. It is black, but muddy from the wet red desert. I doubt the driver can see us, and I'm thankful.

Gardner watches it, taut and wary, until it's a speck on the horizon. It's only when he relaxes that I stroke Freya's cheek and whisper to her that it's time to wake up. She stirs and shivers.

"I'm cold."

I hug her to me and fold her little fingers around the saved piece of jerky. "Here. Come on, let's start down."

2

FAULK

I shake out my sleeping bag and sand grains flick into my face.

"Shit!"

I rub my eyes, making it worse. It's cold, and the rain has obliterated their tracks.

I figure they've already worked out something's going down. Just wish I didn't have to drive this noisy pile of crap. Battery powered at least folks, come on! But that wasn't an option, apparently.

I curl into a tight ball and pull the bag up around my chin to get warmer. Could I leave the vehicle behind? Would I be fast enough? Maybe. She has the child; I just have myself. I contemplate a night like this out in the open and decide to leave the decision to dump it until tomorrow.

The moon shines in the back window, right into my eyes. *Go to sleep, bitch.* She whites me out. I turn over and close my eyes. Sleep eludes me for an hour, maybe more, but then I'm drifting down, the absolute silence of the desert hashing in my ears.

The dawn sun is bright and harsh. Childhood cool and misty days float beneath my eyelids and I wish I didn't have to wake. I could turn back, back to the Dome and the just-rightness of the city, forget what they asked of me, forget that I'd pretended to care but didn't, really. I don't; it's a job, like any other. Leave the right and the wrong of it to them.

I get up, and emerge from the car into a desert pooled with water; eyes that reflect the sky in a thousand small splices across the land. My pile of metal glints in the brightness and I know I can't leave her yet. When I run out of fuel—that rare and strange petroleum they bestowed upon me as though it were a flask of liquid gold—then I'll leave her to the sun and rain to rust and die like the fossil she is.

I get back in, crank up the engine and begin searching for their traces between the puddles.

HIS DINING ROOM is yellow today. Last week it was red. An improvement, maybe, but it doesn't seem to have improved Goldengass's mood. The colour gives his skin a greenish hue. Or maybe it's just the old interface. Or the desert dust that layers everything here.

"How can they still be ahead of you? You have a car for crying out loud, they've only got legs."

Only legs. Guess I should expect this from a man who chooses to confine himself to a chair. A suffocating life. I gaze out at the wide, pink sky through my windscreen. *How can he stand it?* Now I'm out here, I wonder how I did.

"Parker, can you hear me?"

"Yes."

"Well?"

"This thing's like a herd of wildebeest. They can hear me a mile away."

"Then ditch it."

"Gladly. When I've run out of fuel."

"Just ditch it Parker. You afraid of being on foot out there?" He waves a buttered bun at me. "What the hell did I choose you for if you can't spend a night outdoors?"

Good question. Why the hell did *he choose me?*

"You've got three days. After that, I'm bringing you in. Get someone else out there who knows how to do their job."

I switch him off before he can sign out. Petty, yes, but I'm not above petty.

It's like it never rained. The sparkling puddles have soaked into the thirsty ground. The sky blazes wide as the sun slaps its heat at me through the window to get me moving.

I start up the car again. Just a bit further. We're kinda like friends now, me and the rust bucket. She can take me for a bit longer. I don't have their tracks, but I think I've worked out where they're heading. Goldengass could pile on the action at the Dome gates and bring them in, do my work for me. But that'd be a gamble. They're not going to walk straight in. Might slink up the river; wait until night to take the back way in. Or maybe I've got them wrong and they're not heading to the city at all.

As I drive across crust and saltbush, I wonder what it'd be like to live out here. It wouldn't be all bad. No shit-piling bureaucrats. None of the 'we're all in this together' bullshit. You could do what you want. Be who you want. If you could find water, food, shelter. That put a dampener on things really. But people did it. There were still folk out here. Farmers who refused to leave their land, claiming that they'd weathered generations of drought and flood and were just going to keep on doing it. Of course, the subsidies dried up long ago. You're a lunatic now, no longer a battler, if you stay out on the land.

I think about the long Retreat. Haven't thought about it for years. The tripling of the city's population as the desert invaded the arable land, and they moved in from all quarters of the state. It had happened to the other cities too. There'd been the arguments over how far to extend the Domes—who to include, who to leave out. The rallies, anger on the streets. I'd been too young to get it. But there were a few years there where you just didn't go out after dark—kids didn't go anywhere without their parents. If you had that kind of parent, that is.

It'd settled down, eventually. Highly touted architectural and cultural solutions created a new sense of space in the high-density city environment. We learnt at school—it was drummed into us—how interdependent we all were, how the mistakes of our forefathers had brought us to this impasse; that we owed the land, owed each other. But it was too little, too late. I didn't feel it. Any of it. Felt only anger. They couldn't even claim ignorance. They just weren't the ones who had to live with it.

It happens sooner than I expect. We kangaroo-hop and then she splutters to a stop. Just when I'd decided to name her. *Well, that's it, your days are done, old girl.* I get my things together slowly, trying to keep my pack as light as possible without leaving something potentially life-saving behind. I call it essential preparation, but I know it's procrastination. Motivation is low right now.

"Goodbye Scrap."

I give her a pat on the bonnet. She looks forlorn as I walk away, already a relic of an old world, wedged in the sand, left to age with the New Desert.

I give them more credit now. The sun is relentless, radiating heat from both sky and sand. *How'd she get a child to walk so far?* I've already drunk two-thirds of the water in my bottle, and despite the recent rain, there's not a drop to be seen now. I wonder if moving at night'd be a better option.

I find their tracks at last. The woman's are medium-sized, with a fairly even stride length and a good, firm footing. Next to hers run the child's. Sometimes she walks, sometimes she scampers, and occasionally I can see where she's been picked up and carried for a while. No wonder, as the child's expending at least double the energy of the woman as she circles interesting shrubs, picks up stones, drops them, runs off several metres to the east or west and then runs back again.

Their tracks make them human. I begin to imagine them as the people they must be. The usual feeling sinks into my gut; the paradox. The beginning of that connection I need to make. I'd always likened it to the hunting of other animals, to the work of the sport shooter or game manager...but now, with this vast landscape to hold and clarify my thoughts, I begin to doubt it. Maybe it was like that once, long ago, when we really needed to bring down prey to eat. But not now. You don't need to feel the water in their blood, the life in their tracks, the way the air moves between hunter and hunted. The gear and the gun: thinking it makes you a big man. It doesn't, it makes you smaller. I know that. With every death, I am diminished.

The dog's prints run fairly straight beneath both their tracks, though sometimes I see them circle back or see an imprint of its behind as it sits and waits for them. I wonder what it's sniffing out that allows it to stay ahead of them, as though it's leading them, instead of the other way around. After a while, I begin to see a pattern in its movements.

"Darn it, clever mutt."

They crest each rise, run along the rocky ridge for a while and come down at seemingly random points; run back on themselves and then loop forward in the same direction. I lose them almost every time they come off a ridge and it takes time to find their tracks again. Finally, I've learnt my lesson and I don't follow them up the next rise, but circle it, looking to pick up the tracks again from the base.

I find them eventually and follow them out over boulder country for the next several hours. I can't see anyone ahead, but an army of granite tors stretches between me and the horizon and any one of them might be a figure in the distance.

The circuitous route has lost me valuable time, and the sun is resting golden in the west before I decide to quit and make camp. With the little one, she'll surely have to stop too. The rocks like standing stones loom between us and I feel strangely less alone knowing my quarry is out there under the eyes of these giants too.

I wake before dawn to something tugging at me in my sleep, an urgency to get moving. Rolling up my sleeping mat, I feel a twinge in my right hip, reminding me it's been a while since I camped out. But the night was kind to me: dark, with a clouded moon, no wind and no dew.

I pull open a tin of beans, eat them cold, and then lug my pack onto my back as the sun slices out across the horizon. I walk along their tracks. An early morning raven has already strutted across their path.

Eventually, I reach an arena of haphazardly strewn boulders. The woman and her kid camped the night here. They even made a fire, its glow shielded from me, tucked under a leaning stone. The coals are cold.

I look around. This was occupied land once. First by the

old people, then by the new; the hopeful, the destroyers. And now it's kept by no-one. The desert's fingers press hard here, but I can see evidence of greener days: a metal cattle trough, rusted through, sits absurd and askew on the red sand; a hopeful opening to the sky. I walk over to it and see a little pool of water in one corner. I try and scoop some into my bottle. Not much goes in, but it's better than none. As I turn back around, my boot topples a pile of small stones: a recent creation; by the girl, no doubt. I bend down and rebuild the tiny cairn, wondering how long it will stand against the wind and shifting sand. I pick off the top stone: a smooth, flat, round one; orange, with an inner ring of yellow, and drop it into my pocket.

Next, I scan the circumference of the fire, searching for their direction. It's been swept clean. Looks like she used a rug or sleeping bag. I wonder why she bothered, as I pick up their tracks a little way along, through an opening amongst the boulders.

They travel straight today. The girl gets carried more often. They seem to be hurrying, no doubt because of me. It's a funny thing, knowing even as you bear your quarry no personal malice that they are right to run from you.

I put my head down too, beginning to weary of this hunt. I know enough about them now and anything extra just makes the job more difficult. I'm not one for that kind of challenge. I like sweet and clean. Job done.

It occurs to me they must be travelling some distance by night to be keeping ahead of me. I examine their tracks more closely and see where nocturnal creatures have crossed them: a dunnart, a hopping mouse, a rabbit. Of course, the fire had long gone cold. They were probably walking half the night. I kick a rock. Fool me for thinking that you couldn't push a child for so long.

Two raptors are circling just ahead. As I walk, I watch them dip and soar off, their wings barely moving as the desert thermals carry them across the sky. If I could only see what they see...I look down at the ground and I can't even see my feet as my eyes adjust from the squint and glare. I stop, drink some water. No sleep for me tonight then. I hope for straight tracks and a full white moon to see by.

GOLDENGASS IS out of his chair, pacing from side to side, making sharp U-turns at the edges of my interface.

"Parker, I don't think you understand the urgency. They are a threat, to our security, to all we hold dear, to all we've accomplished. I don't want them a step closer. Of course they're headed for the city! But you're not going to let them get this far."

His face goes pale when he rages. I'd expected red, but it must be all those years of training. Emotions turned inwards, eating him up from the inside. Heart disease or cancer; I'd lay my bets on one of them to finish him off. He's probably already riddled through and doesn't even know it.

"Okay."

"Okay. Good."

He signs out. The silence is a beautiful thing.

I'D BEEN PREPARED for a night of walking, but I hadn't been prepared for this. From the distance I took it for just another pile of boulders. Now I'm sitting in the dust outside a dwelling cut from rock and earth, in front of a bright yellow door painted with lush green botanical designs and hung with a rust-red bell. Their trail brought me here, to this absurdly bright and hopeful door. I explore all around the outside of the house. Vehicle tracks lead out from a locked garage. I could knock again, ring the bell, but I know they're not here. There is no one here.

It takes me a while, but I reason that if there's a dwelling, there must be a road nearby. I begin to follow the vehicle tracks, hoping they'll lead me to bitumen sooner rather than later. *Dammit, Scrap, I could do with you now.*

It's only an hour before I reach the road. It is long and straight and empty. I walk along the city-bound side and place my order. It's another half an hour before a platoon slides quietly up beside me. There are only three cars in the string, all empty. Not much cause for travel along this road these days. The last one is a carrier, packed with steel boxes bound for the Dome. I get into the first car, chuck my pack behind me and strap myself in. The seat is soft. I crank up the air con, lean back and close my eyes.

3

ANNA

*G*ardner stalks, muzzle to ground ahead of us. Freya is enlivened by her night's sleep and runs splashing from puddle to puddle. I've given up worrying about wet shoes; they'll dry well enough in the days to come as the desert heats up once more to scorching.

We heard the car again this morning, off to the east. Freya is getting used to the sound. She's curious about the noise and I try to explain, as much as I know, about how people moved around in old times before she was born. I'm sure Gardner could add more accurate details to my story, but she gets the picture. What fascinates her is not the strangeness of the vehicle itself, but that it might carry only one person, and that the same person could drive it. She likes the idea, and she drives Gardner, pulling on his ears to steer him. He races with her on his back, splashing in and out of the shallow pools, and she clings to him, shrieking with laughter.

I allow myself to breathe, will myself to enjoy the unaccustomed freshness on my face and my daughter's joy, but I can't release the foreboding that circles within me like my blood.

We've been out here for a fortnight, but it feels like years. My girl, like a desert pearl washed up far from home, is running now. I wonder where she gets her energy. Her legs are strong and her face is brown with sun and dirt.

My own mother must have watched me like this in the days of my growing up, when we were always moving. The land wouldn't allow us to stay long. There was little to sustain us, but if we kept walking, we could find enough berries and tubers, snakes and rabbits to keep us well. Solar packs and portable wind turbines gave us power. Satellites were no longer accessible to all, so our devices became useless and we had to rediscover other ways to navigate and communicate. Our way of life was a deliberate return to nomadism. My mother's people, in a fervour of idealism, had chosen to reinvent their lives during the Retreat, to turn their backs on city life. We still traded with the Dome for flour and clothing. We were travelling artisans; the new gypsies, treated with both romanticism and contempt by the residents of the Dome. Some of us carried memory of an older way of living on country, and these remnants of knowledge and dreamings passed down from elders helped. It was enough to sustain us, but not enough to become truly independent in this changed landscape.

Several years ago, many of us began to weary of travel and envisaged an easier way of life. In an ironic echoing of the Dome, we built curved structures, half below ground, inspired by the underground houses of the abandoned opal-mining town of Coober Pedy. Not all of us chose to live this way; some ancestral stories of underworld spirits kept a number of us moving on. But my mother stayed. She was getting older and needed a place to rest.

I left my mother two weeks ago in her cool burrow furnished with woven throws and desert stones. She had begun a garden—a square space outside her kitchen, lit by a shaft of light from above. We had stood beneath that skylight, inhaling the damp mint smell of the newly mulched rock ferns, and I had hugged her strong, brown body. She had a red scarf tied around her long grey hair. Her eyes had crinkled and warmed as I said goodbye. She was content, and that had given me the strength to go.

WE WALK LONG into the nights, and each day, Gardner has us up before the sun.

He nudges me awake gently. I never begrudge being awoken early, though sleep is dear to me. What is dearer is the chance to watch him during the shift. It takes only a murk of pre-dawn light to awaken his cells to his daytime form. As the first kookaburra calls the end of night, he takes off his clothing and sits still, facing east. For years I longed to see his human face meet the morning sun. But it is always the dingo who greets the day with a howl.

Sunset is the only time he feels sunlight on his skin, and he soaks in it until the last red rays are done. Only then will he dress and ready himself for the night as a man.

We sweep the evidence of his human footprints away from our campsite, as we have done every morning. I can't see much in the gloom, and hope I haven't missed any. I strap Freya onto my back, lift my backpack onto my front and follow Gardner as he picks his way through the looming boulders. He pulls us through the day. We eat as we walk and I rarely put Freya down. She doesn't complain much; I think she's grateful for the rest. The weight of my pack balances her weight against my back. I feel strong today.

By afternoon, I let Freya run and Gardner seems a little less harried. We rest beside each other. We've stopped for a break and some water. I trickle some into my palm and he licks it up. I watch the side of his face and try to see into him, to the man inside. He stops drinking, lifts his head, and goes back to watching our daughter. I wonder, not for the first time, exactly what he sees.

After a moment—too soon—he stands up and turns to me. I nod.

"Let's go, sweetheart."

Freya is drawing patterns with a stick. She doesn't look up. I walk over, take her free hand.

"Come on, we have to go."

She shakes her head. I look at what she has drawn. Three figures in the sand. A woman, a girl and a dog. With circles and circles and circles around them. I bend down and look into her eyes.

"Is that us?"

She nods. "The circles keep us safe."

I bring her little body into a hug. "Okay."

She shakes me off and starts up another circle around the rest.

"Possum, we need to get moving."

She shakes her head again.

"No, Mummy, I need to make more circles."

I let her make another, and then another, until finally Gardner goes to her and lowers himself to the ground. She climbs onto his back, still clutching her stick, and buries her face into his fur.

GARDNER

No one can hurt you.

I speak words to my daughter that arise and fade only in the dark space of my mind. I know she can't hear them, but I always hope she can feel them. Her knees dig into my ribs. It doesn't hurt; but she's taller, stronger than she's ever been, and her weight on my back slows me more than it used to. I wonder how much longer I'll be able to carry her; how many more years. One day, perhaps sooner than I can fathom right now, she won't want me to carry her anymore. *Freya. Do you know? How can you know? Do you know that I would carry you for a thousand years?*

Her mother is up ahead. Anna; sometimes such a fire-brand, but today not so; simply strong, full of mothering energy and purpose. I'd have all the ways she is: I'd take her smarts, her worry, her calm and her fire. She shifts and flickers like a flame that ever turns with the air that blows it and the fuel that it consumes. She's always been wary of her father's quicksilver nature; his temper, his ferocious embrace of his passion of the moment, whether an idea or a thing, and I know that she feels a fight against it within herself. But she is mercurial in ways unlike her father, in ways she cannot herself see.

Today, I sense more of her mother in her. We've spent so much time of late in Elma's calm, wise presence that I miss her in the way it must be to miss one's own mother. I almost envy that Anna can count on her mother's love; how she has used it well, as a framework upon which to build a life; as she should have; as Freya is also building. A makeshift, sinewy thing is all I have made. It suits me well enough, but to have had a heart built for me and to rest within the peace of that...*ah Anna, what a treasure you possess.*

Anna and Freya are my treasures. My world. And that's all right with me.

We walk until it seems that we're not walking but that the world is flowing towards us; the whole, wide landscape throwing itself at us as though it's hungry for company. If loneliness had a scent, it would be this acrid smell of dry grass and baking dust.

For the last hour we've traversed low, rolling country. The clusters of grey boulders that accompanied our passage all day are becoming rarer, so I guess that the silhouette I see in the distance now is no standing stone. I raise my nose to the faint breeze. It is a dwelling. And there are people; I'm sure of it. Moist earth, cooking oil and a subtle sting of chilli perfumes the air. I yelp softly to Anna. She squints ahead, hand shielding the sun from her eyes. Then she sees it too and catches my gaze in wonder. I howl to warn Freya, who clutches my fur more tightly as we pick up our pace.

4

ANNA

I find our unexpected hosts remarkable.

Only hours before, we'd stumbled wearily to their door and they'd offered us a lift without questions or hesitation.

In their car, the woman, Meiying, holds cups under the drinks outlet and dispenses mineralised water for us all, while the man, Renshu, hands us fresh fruit. Then he starts up the engine and begins to drive. I try not to convey my nervousness as he takes the controls. Freya eats her mandarin in wide-eyed silence and Gardner sits up on the back seat, his face turned towards the window. I sit between them both and take a moment to look out too as I crunch down on my second apple for the week. It takes me some time to process the view of the desert flashing by at such speed; I realise I've become accustomed to the more natural pace of our walking.

Renshu is talking, answering my questions. Meiying doesn't say much, but there is a synchronous energy between them: the feather touch of hand on knee, a smile of acknowledgement at a comment or gesture.

"Yes, there are a few of us out here. Sometimes we get together, rarely; just often enough to remind ourselves that we're not alone. Our nearest neighbours are the Clapshaws. They're an old farming family who've been out here longer than us. They keep a few chooks and even a horse."

The purloined saddle-rug sticks out from the top of my backpack. I try not to look at it.

"So, how did you all come to live out so far from the Dome?"

"We're part of an experiment, for the triple L."

"The triple...?"

"The LLL, the Long Life League. We're both cancer survivors. The LLL is studying the effects of life-extension therapy on people in long-term cancer remission. They're comparing those who live in the Dome with those in an electromagnetism-reduced environment. We were in the group chosen for minimal exposure to EMFs. So, they sent us out here, away from the Dome. We drive our car—can't do driverless of course—once a fortnight to a get our supplies, just outside the Dome. They pay for everything." He pushes his gold-framed glasses back up his nose and I hope one hand on the steering wheel is enough.

Renshu's hair is mostly grey, with hints of the dark colour it must once have been, but his skin is smooth and brown. His eyes are black and the glasses magnify small smile lines around the corners.

"How long have you both been cancer-free then...that is, if you don't mind me asking?"

They look at each other and smile.

"For me, 24 years this month and Meiying's coming up to 26 years."

Freya is getting restless beside me, kicking her feet against the seat.

"I'm almost five. How old are you?" She directs her question to Meiying.

Meiying smiles at Freya with eyes like dark gems. "I am 92 and Renshu is 89 years old." Her voice is peaceful in the way the surface of a deep river is peaceful. "But almost five— what a special age to be, such a big girl, so clever."

Freya beams. Even Gardner turns to look at Meiying, and I find I'm shaking my head from side to side.

"Wow, so it's working."

Meiying nods. "It appears to be."

"How far are we taking you?" asks Renshu. "Do you want to go all the way to the Border Market with us? Then you won't be too far from the Dome gate."

I look at Gardner and see consent in his eyes.

"Thank you, that'd be great."

The talk dies down after that. Freya lays her head on my lap and closes her eyes. Gardner remains watchful at the window and I allow my mind to wander languidly with the landscape. For the moment, it seems, we are safe.

As the shadows lengthen and the land speeds by, flat and uninhabited, I begin to worry that the sun will set before we reach the border. Gardner is no longer still; he shifts and twitches beside me and I know he would be pacing if he could.

"Not far now," says Meiying.

"We get our staples there," says Renshu, "We have a big meal, camp overnight, buy our produce in the morning and then drive home. If you can find a place to stay, you can get some delicious things early on, before the city folk arrive."

Finally, we stop. The night market is a sparkling serpent in the swale below us. Renshu opens the doors for us and unloads our packs. Meiying presses more fruit into my hands.

"Safe journey," she says to me, "I hope you find what you are seeking."

I bow my head; it seems the only thing to do. I gave them no explanation, no story. I thank her, thank them both. I want to stay with them, within their accepting warmth, their bubble of hope and luck. Freya feels it too, though she could not name it. She stands by Gardner's side, strangely forlorn.

Meiying goes to her, kneels so that she's at Freya's height. Freya's face is small and serious as Meiying takes her hands into her own.

"These hands will grow. But your heart—it is already big and bright." She gives Freya a hug and stands up.

They get back into the car, waving, and drive down the hill and away.

We are standing beneath a spreading red gum with a massive, rough trunk and fallen limbs all around. Gardner settles on the other side of it where the sun's dying light will turn his fur to bare skin.

I sit Freya on my lap and let her have a feed of milk. She drinks, but she's distracted. Her gaze is drawn to the lights below. She finishes quickly and I console myself that for the first time in many days, she can have some good, solid food.

When Gardner emerges, Freya jumps up and runs to him.
"Daddy!"

He pulls her into his arms and breathes into her hair.
"My beautiful girl."

There is nothing canine about his human face, about the bright blue eyes that smile at me in the last light of the day as he holds Freya to him, or the clean-shaven face that I suspect he keeps so to accentuate the difference between the man and the dog. I see him anew each evening.

His arms around me now are warm and strong. Freya nudges in between us, and we lift her up for a kiss. Then the three of us walk down the hill together.

The night market is vast. Glowing tents sit side by side, issuing a sizzle and clang of woks and pots and plates of steaming food. Smoke and red sparks rise into the darkening sky. We keep close to each other as we enter through a gap between the stalls. Freya's eyes are wide in the lantern light and she grips my hand tightly.

"Let's get something to eat, shall we?" I talk into her ear so she can hear me above the clamour of cooking.

Gardner stays close by her other side as I lead us into a stall. I order a serve of Mee Goreng and a meat dish for Gardner and we move to a table in the shadows. We all eat quickly; I'm so hungry that I can't stop to savour the hot food in my mouth. Our stomachs fill quickly and Freya is soon holding her hands to her belly and complaining of the pain. I can't blame her for having eaten so much so quickly, but I should have warned her. Gardner takes her onto his lap and she snuggles in.

I watch the tables fill around us. People eating quickly, talking loudly. I wonder if Renshu and Meiying are nearby. Gardner places his hand over mine. He looks tired. I hadn't noticed the strain on his face by the light of our nightly fires, but here I can see him more clearly.

"I think we should camp away from the crowds tonight. We need a good rest before tomorrow. What do you think?"

I'm caught short by his question. He has been making most of the decisions for us since we began. I pour some water into a glass.

"You don't think we'd be safe enough surrounded by all these people?"

He shrugs.

"I don't know."

I'm so used to trusting his canine instincts that I don't expect him not to know. A flash of heat prickles my skin and my heart begins to thump. The market seems to press in all around me, loud and bright. I breathe, trying to settle an urge to grab Freya and run. Gardner is watching me. She is curled up against him, her head tucked into his chest, almost asleep.

"How about back up the hill? Then we can see anything coming."

He nods and closes his eyes. "Good."

We have just pushed our chairs back to leave when we hear the first scream. A woman runs past our marquee, her face contorted in fright, her long, dark hair flying out behind her. I see a blur of red—her clothes I think—but I can't help imagining blood. Her screaming is subsumed by a swell of voices, shouting, confused. Freya, awakened and eyes wide with shock, begins to cry. Gardner holds her and shushes her. People jump up from their tables. The crowd presses in and I see others running towards us, calling out, as if harried by something from behind. Then a bright floodlight from above, accompanied by a dark roar of rotor blades, has us all shielding our faces. Gardner pulls me down, grasps my hand, and leads us towards a slit in the marquee's canvas. We slip through and begin to run.

We race along behind the tents, tripping over guy ropes and boxes until Gardner leads us up the hill. The gap between us widens—Gardner is so much faster than me on the slope, even with Freya in his arms. She's still crying and I want to quieten her, to tell her it'll be all right. He stops to let me catch up. I wave him on. He races up the hill, holding Freya tight to his chest.

He crests the rise before I do. The ridge is flooded with a

bright, broad spotlight beam, and I see Gardner and Freya starkly visible at its centre. Then the lights glare into my eyes. I dive to the ground, flatten myself against the slope and crush my face into the grass and dirt. There's shouting from above me, from several men, in at least two directions, and Freya's crying stops abruptly.

I look, even though I know my face will glow white in the spotlight beam if it passes across me. I see cars—Silk Moths I'm sure—and men silhouetted, like a troop of black insects at work; struggling, roping, lifting; carrying the limp forms of Freya and Gardner away from me.

A great roar rises within me and I want to charge them, beat them down. But my body won't move. I am frozen against the side of the hill. The lights sink below the rise and fade away. I don't know how long I remain prostrate, shivering, clutching at the earth. Eventually, I try to get up, but I'm retching and vomiting and I can't move myself from the filth. Can only sit there, rocking and wailing. They're gone. Gone. The night is dark after the glare. The feeble lights of the market below me dwindle and narrow in front of my eyes until all I can see is black.

5

FAULK

*B*loody Goldengass. I want the interface to be more than air; I want to punch it and hit something solid.

"You'll still get your pay, Parker." Contempt drips like drool from his sagging mouth. I close him down. I'm angry, I'm hungry and I need a friggin' shower.

I stalk along the line of tents. People are back to business now, cooking meals for the late-night punters, most of whom are pissed, refuelling after a night out in the Dome. They'll go back there before sunrise, like vampires to their dens. I won't return tonight. It's not like there's anyone waiting there for me. Except Goldengass. The rat shit of a man.

I want to make him sweat, to wonder what I'm doing, whether I'll come back for the debrief at all. If it wasn't for the dollars, I wouldn't. I'd take my secrets and sell them.

I decide to deal with the hunger first; duck into a stall and order a dish of something sizzling and hot. It comes quickly and I sit in a corner and scoff it down. It's a testament to Goldengass's power that the police aren't swarming all over the place; you wouldn't know there'd been a raid if you hadn't been here. I hunker down, trying to find calm. I still my breathing and open my senses to my surroundings. Beyond the drunken laughter at the next table, I can hear the piping and chirping of insects in the grass. I look out along the side of the tent up to the dark rise behind. A huge eucalypt stretches out pale ghost limbs against the night sky.

I am full and tired. The sounds of humanity all around me feel like a physical assault. I get up and head off into the night. The glow of the eucalypt draws me up the hill. I'll find a camp spot on the other side. I climb through the grass, my boots like bricks, my limbs slow. The food is heavy in my stomach and I need to pee. I stop to take a slash, feeling the relief, hearing cicadas and the growing peace of the night. It takes a moment to register the other sound. A low, moaning wail, coming from somewhere across the slope.

I finish up, scramble towards the sound and almost trip over something dark and solid on the ground. Too soft to be a rock. I bend down. There's someone there, huddled and rocking back and forth. I can smell vomit. Just a drunk kid. I get up to go, but a hand grabs my leg.

"Don't..."

I try to shake it off, but the grip is strong and nails bite into my skin.

"Don't leave." Sounds like a woman.

I bend down again.

"Okay."

She releases her grip.

I try to lift her up. Her legs buckle.

"Come on, up you get."

She stands up this time. I flop her arm around my neck

like it's a scarf and start heading down the hill with her. She cries out.

"No. Not that way. No. No." She is shaking her head like a maniac.

I turn around and drag her up the hill. As we near the top, she starts shivering and I take more of her weight onto my shoulders, stagger past the tree and down to a flat place that'll do to make camp. I dump her in the grass and chuck a rug from my pack over her while I collect enough dead wood for a fire.

After it's lit, I look across. She's been quiet since I put her down. The firelight glows on her sleeping face. I see long, reddish hair, dark eyelashes, a thin, brown body plastered with dirt. Something is tugging at me. I try to still my sleep-deprived mind as I watch her body rise and fall. Something...

Then it clicks.

It's her.

So Goldengass only got the kid. I try and calculate how much this'll raise my fee. How much is she worth on her own? Do I bring her in tonight or wait until morning? My head aches. Too many thoughts are slithering around in there, and I need some sleep.

I haul a log onto the fire and watch sparks sail up into the sky. I rub my temples and watch her through the smoke. She won't be moving any time soon. I yawn. Tomorrow. I'll think it all through tomorrow.

6

ANNA

I wake to an unfamiliar sound. A loud click and a metallic chink. I don't open my eyes. The sun is already bright. I don't move. I want to think. I've awoken to a pain in my chest; the wound where Freya and Gardner were ripped from me. Each question tightens my heart further. Are they alive? Are they together? Is she afraid? To hold all this in my mind is to hold something within me that is burning—I want to fling the white-hot thing away, throw away the reality. But I can't let fear immobilise me again. I need to move and act today.

I'm not where I left them. It comes back in hazy fragments. A stranger lifting me, carrying me here. Wherever here is. I fight the impulse to open my eyes. I'm not ready yet. First, I need to think out a plan.

It isn't much of one, but it's a goal at least. The Dome. The only place they can be. I have to get in. Renshu and Meiying—their car with no wireless, no tracking. I have to find their campground. I hear the noise again and keep my body still as I open my eyes and catch a flash of something

39

silver disappearing into a large coat pocket. A man is sitting on the other side of a white charcoal firepit, packing his things.

I haven't moved, but he looks across at me.

"Morning. Feeling better?"

I open and close my mouth; my tongue fuzzy with dehydration. He throws a water bottle across to me and I sit up, my whole body stiff and aching, and take a drink. The water is cold from the night and it makes me shiver. I sit the bottle in the dirt, pull myself fully upright and gather the blanket into my lap. I can feel him watching me.

"Thank you." I start pulling off pieces of dry grass and squaring the dirt-stained material into neat folds.

"No trouble. You hungry?"

He pulls out a packet of something that looks like dry cereal. I'm not. I shake my head. He shrugs and begins eating straight out of the bag.

I stand up. His gaze follows me. I point off behind a couple of shrubs. I need to pee. As I squat, angled so that I'm hidden from him, the hot fluid hits the ground and a pang of panic rips at me. I can't be here, alive and doing something so normal while Freya and Gardner are not. I'm shaking as I hurry back to the camp, the renewed urgency and fear liquid in my gut.

My backpack must still be on the slope somewhere, so I have nothing to take with me. I wonder if I can retrieve it on my way down. I wait until my hands have stopped shaking and then pick up the folded rug and hand it to him.

"Thanks," I say again. He takes it and I turn towards the hill.

"Whoa, wait. Where are you going?"

"I have to go back."

"I'm going the same way." He shrugs his pack onto his

shoulders. "Here." He passes me a bar of chocolate. I take it, nodding, and stash in a pocket. I can't face food.

We trudge past the giant eucalypt and I feel as though someone has poked me with a hot iron as I think of Gardner sitting so calmly at its base barely twelve hours ago. My heart races again as panic threatens to overwhelm me. I try to breathe, that's all. To breathe enough to continue on. The part of me that is alert to my daughter, to her slightest cry, her every movement, is seeking her, listening for her. I'm like a rubber band stretched so taut it threatens to snap as I scan the land behind me and the invisible city before me, searching for her.

He slows his pace to stay by my side. I imagine it's kindness, but I need him gone. Need to find a way to walk against the heavy hand that is pressing me back.

I start down the hill, but he grabs my arm.

"Not that way, too many sweeper bots."

"What?"

"The raid on the market last night. Sweeper bots'll be out for the journos. Don't know about you but I'm not up for being photographed right now."

I shake my head and allow him to guide me across the slope so that we come down outside the entrance of the market. Two women emerge with baskets of greens. It's been a long time since I've seen Dome residents. Their clothes spangle and refract in the sunlight and I guess the fabric must be embedded with glimmer solar cells, something that had just become popular before I left. They both have short hair, with pins in the shape of green leaves. Their faces are smooth and brown, skin glowing with youth and vigour. They glance at me, a quick up and down, and walk on—how I must seem to them, a ragged apparition from the dust.

Others file out, heading Domeward, each one slim, clean

and glittering. They don't talk to each other; most are engaged in virtual dialogue, or simple cloud watching, of the plugged-in kind. Not one of them would think to look up at the actual sky.

I look back at my companion; he doesn't fit either, a man of dirt and hard ground. He's been watching me watching them. Now he raises his eyebrows.

"Tossers."

I actually laugh. It's a strange, horsey sound that doesn't belong to me, and it's followed by another wrench of panic, this time edged with guilt. I try to take a deep breath and, as I glance at him again, I find him staring.

"What's your name?" I ask, as much to give myself a moment that's mine, as anything else; to throw the spotlight's glare on him.

"Faulk. Faulk Parker...yours?"

"Anna."

"You heading into the city?" The fact that he doesn't call it the Dome betrays that he's from there. Anything outside the Dome barely registers to most of them; it's wasteland, long ago relegated to memory—the residents of our capital cities don't like to think of themselves as cossetted; they think they're the free ones.

"I need to go to the campground. I've got friends there waiting for me."

He raises his eyebrows but lets the lie pass. "This way then."

I immediately regret telling him where I'm headed; he seems to have taken my protection as his personal duty.

We walk along the path leading away from the market. It swings upwards along the face of the hill on the opposite side of the swale. We trudge up the gravel track, my legs feeling tired and heavy. Finally, we reach the top.

As we climb up onto the ridge, I find myself gasping from more than the exertion. The Great Southern Dome lies beneath us, extraordinary in its breadth and alien in its beauty. It is white with a tinge of rose in the morning light, a thing of air and cloud. From here, I can appreciate for the first time that it truly is a cocoon. A web of spun silk. Designed by human architects, constructed by genetically engineered silkworms; the entire dome made from nature's miracle fibre, reinforced, and implanted with solar cells. It makes me wonder what new and malignant creature might emerge from such a thing. For emerge we must. It's not like humanity to hide away for long.

Faulk Parker is also looking down on his city. His stillness reminds me of Gardner.

I try to feel into the Dome, reach in and find them. I wonder if I would feel it if they died. I hope I'd know, somehow. Hope beyond possibility that I would know.

I'm suddenly impatient and stride down towards the campground and the city. My companion falls into step behind me. I no longer care. I just need to keep moving toward them.

7

FAULK

I didn't actually expect her to know anyone at the campground, but she is walking with purpose amongst the tents, searching for someone. I hang back a bit. She's getting jumpy with my constant presence. Like the cat that relaxes in your arms only to leap away as soon as you loosen your grip, I get the feeling she'll try and slip off soon.

She stops at a car and looks in at the passenger window. It has a steering wheel. She tries the door, but it's locked. She paces, looking off against the glare, until it's clear there's no one around. Then she deflates, like she's become an empty sack, and sits heavily on the grass.

"You go. I'm going to wait."

I sit down next to her, arms over my tented knees. Casual.

"I can get you into the city."

"What makes you think I need that?" Her voice is sharp.

"You're waiting by a trackless car."

"I'm waiting for my friends."

It's been the finest of balancing acts, and now I have to

step a little further off the line than I'd like. I hope I'm making the right play.

"Suit yourself."

I get up and start to walk away. I can feel her following me with her gaze. I lengthen my stride.

"Wait!"

Now I'm the cat. I smile as I turn around.

WE CLIMB up to sit knee to knee in a compact car in a long platoon bound for the city. People and produce are piled into cars behind and in front of us. I enter my ID, sign in for two passengers with the city centre as our destination. She's twitchy, one knee jiggling, hands fidgeting in her lap as she looks out the window. In the trapped air of the car I can smell us; that outdoor odour of lichen, smoke, and sweat. It's not unpleasant, just so organic against the perfumed air deodoriser and the more ominous undertow of a new car off-gassing.

I open a vent to let in some air. She takes off her jacket coated with red desert dust. I don't mean to stare, but a patch of wetness is seeping through the fabric at one of her breasts. I'm mesmerised by the rapidly expanding circle. She works out what's happening and grabs the coat, pulls it to her chest, her face reddening and furious. Then she turns to the window and I guess she's probably crying.

I hadn't realised she was still feeding the girl. It shouldn't matter. But I can't help the images rising to the surface now; memories that I know will only mess with me, take my mind off what I need to do. I can't push them down:

Mia's face, shining with sweat and joy; flashes of the blood and fear that brought him to us and the fierce, unbidden pride and protectiveness that opened me up and laid me bare. I only held my son that one time. Held him and knew I'd die for him—just like that—a simple, quiet thing. Not a roar, not violent, just a knowing that here was something that made everything that came before worth it.

I left him there, in Mia's arms, her blue t-shirt stained with birth, her brown arms around him strong and soft. He'd had dark hair, almost black, and lots of it. His eyes were grey and clear and they knew me. I left them for a shower, for clothes and some food.

The hole in the ground where the bomb went off was wider than a city block.

It was a week before anyone was allowed back. I had to see it for myself. I stood at the edge of the pit where the hospital had been and somehow expected to see something that was hers. But behind all the flowers and cards there was just grey rubble and dust. And that became my life.

I look now at the side of this woman's face and try to remind myself that she is a terrorist. That helps. It always helps.

The Dome gates rise either side of us: steel arches bending inwards like whale bones, their surfaces, dark mirrors reflecting the outside back to itself. We both look up as we pass beneath them. The road closes into a tunnel and I get the sensation that we are fleshy worms burrowing our way into a shining apple. Like we don't belong, like we'll cause rot. And it's not just her, it's me as well. I belong on the outside—a keeper, a guardian, maybe even a warrior when I allow myself to feel big about it; but I'm not of this place. That's the price: that I can't buy into the illusion, that paradise will not belong to me.

We are under the city's northern district now. It is so dark that I can easily see her reflection in the window. Her eyes follow each tunnel lamp, as though she's afraid to lose the light.

An interface appears in front of me: Goldengass looming in the dark. I swipe it away quickly. She looks at me. I shrug.

"The man's a pain in the ass."

She is suddenly deer-like, taut, ready to spring.

"Where are we stopping?"

"The Square. That suit you?"

"Fine."

She turns to the window again as light streams back in. We are now within the Dome. The road rises upwards as it joins the multi-level highway running into the heart of the city. Pods layer the sky on either side of us, each one a small version of the Dome, perched on a garden pad like a sugary psyllid case on a leaf. Thousands of homes float on the branch tips of each housing tree. Their white reflections glow in her eyes.

We're nearing the end of the line. My hands are in my pockets. I slowly curl the fingers of my left hand around the restraints and my right around the grip of my ECD. I need to time it with our exit; there's no way Goldengass'll let her take one free step in the city.

The Square looms before us, all angle and tone; an oddly sharp remnant of the old city within the smooth roundness of the new one. The platoon pulls up at street level. A massive screen flickers above us. An aerial view of a rain-forest fades into a picture of a coral reef shimmering behind schools of bright-faced fish. For a moment, the inside of the car glows blue, as though we are underwater too. She looks at me, staring up from some great depth as though she's drowning. I grip the cold metal of the restraints and release the catch on my weapon. The doors click to unlock, the glass releases and slides open.

I'm watching her, so she sees them before I do. Golden-gass's men jump at us as we step out. I reach for her, but she's already running, leaping like a rabbit around the back of the car and across the road. I run after her and they're firing at us—both of us! I yell back at them to hold their fire, but they don't stop.

I keep running. She bounds up the steps of the cathedral while they're dodging traffic and I catch up to her just as she reaches the stain-glass interior doors. We push together and they open easily. As we fall in, we're greeted by a wall of sound: trumpets, tubas, a cymbal clash—an orchestra is playing on the chancel stage, and the audience lining the polished wooden pews is unperturbed by our entry. I follow her as she edges between the liquorice all-sort pillars to an empty spot near the end of a pew. Smart girl. I do the same, treading on a few feet to reach a space along the pew behind her. I wait for the sound of gunshot to bring on the panic, scanning to find an alternative exit for when they all scatter, but the shots don't come and the doors stay closed.

Flutes and strings bring the tempo down and I watch the back of her head. She is still; frozen like a Jacky lizard counting on its camouflage right until the very moment you reach out to grab it.

Then I hear sirens. Shots. Gunfire on the city streets is not something to go unnoticed. A loud bell sounds in the church and the orchestra finally stops playing. People stand up, start up a confused chatter and I go to her and grab her hand.

"Come on! This way."

We push through the crowd, towards the stage and the orchestra in chaos—a mad echidna with bright trombone bristles—and through a side exit. We are in the cathedral's side lane. I feel a kick in the guts as I recognise the place from a brighter day. Mia as a bridesmaid. Can't remember the bride's or groom's name; I was watching only Mia as the old-style photographer made them walk and pose and smile and do it all over again until they'd turned into plasticine figures in a kid's animation and their smiles had become painted-on doll's grins.

I stumble.

Anna lets go of my hand and runs ahead of me. The sandstone laneway is like another tunnel and this time I don't know where I'll come out.

She is quick, quicker than I would have imagined for a woman who has eaten nothing but dust for the last two weeks. I guess the hare is always quick when the fox is at its heels. She is just like that—a hare—all springy and long and unpredictable. I emerge from the lane and see a whip of her red hair as she rounds a corner. The sound of the siren fades and the endorphins kick in. The more I run, the more my body eases into the chase. I am the hunter again. She is ahead of me and I am the hound on her scent. Only she doesn't know it yet. We are tracing a vinelike pattern across the city, crossing broad streets filled with people and silent trams, following small tendrils of laneways off the city's main veins. Goldengass and his gorillas have long lost us and I am flying high on my speed and the nearness of my quarry. I resolve to end it at the next corner.

And then I lose her.

"Shit!" The adrenaline that was so sweet a moment before pumps up my heart rate and pours on the vitriol.

I retrace my steps to the last turnoff. Going more slowly now, I notice glances from the glimmerati—some curious, some disdainful. I get the urge to shove one of them to see if I can get the whole city crowd to fall like dominoes across the street.

Instead, I edge up off the footpath, out of the way of the hurrying masses, and lean against an iron rail that cordons off some steps to a garret below street level.

She lunges at me like a funnel-web out of its hole and pushes me to the ground. Then she smashes her hand over my mouth and gets up close to my face.

"Who are you and what the hell do you want with me?"

It occurs to me I've royally messed up, that I'm losing it, losing any touch I ever had in this pathetic game. Goldengass must've known it. Of course he did. Why else would he have sent out the others? It was supposed to be a simple job: bring in a mother, her child and their dog. Hardly taking down a hard-ass assassin; practically domestic duties.

Domestic duties is grabbing me forcefully around the head now.

"Answer me!" She fumbles at my coat pockets and for a disorientating moment, I think she's trying something on. Then I pull myself together and sit up, pushing her off me. She has my restraints, and she's shaking them at me a like a woman who has found lipstick on her husband's collar. "What are these? What the hell are these?"

I reach out and grab them, use them to pull myself up to standing. Unbalanced by my weight, she falls forward into me and I pull the restraints from her hands. I wrangle and drag her so that we're just inside the narrow laneway. I'm angry. Suddenly. It's like an upwelling, an eruption out of nowhere, propelled by my shame, my incompetence. I hold her by the shoulders and shove her against the stone side-wall. She lets out a *whoof* of air and her face turns from anger to shock. I grip her arms and pull her skinny wrists towards me.

"They're..." *click* "for..." *click* "you."

I lift her arms, now locked together by the metal cuffs,

and let go so that they drop heavily against her body. She is looking at me, white with disbelief. I go to grasp her upper arm so I can direct her back out of the alley when she delivers a kick, hard and sharp and right on target between my legs. I double over with a wave of pain and nausea and reach into my pocket...but it's not there. She's squatting in front of me, my weapon shaking in her hands. The last thing I see is her face, lips pressed hard together, eyes glaring at me like a bush owl. And then my world is pain.

8

ANNA

I didn't expect the smell of burnt flesh. Or the convulsions. He falls heavily, face forward and writhing onto the cobblestones. Once I'm far enough away and my hands have stopped their shocked trembling, I begin to feel the first shreds of remorse and hope that someone will find him soon.

I stop, finally, in the sheltered entranceway to a large, grey building that must be an office tower because it's too old to be a housing tree and there are no pods floating above me. The floor beneath me is cold stone. I close my eyes and try to open the hearing of my heart, to feel for my daughter in the city's undertow. But the voice that is hers and that cries out for me comes from within, from my own hurt and fear, and it blocks out everything else.

My eyes snap open. Someone is approaching; I can hear the soft scudding of their shoes. Not Faulk Parker, and not the police. It's a city dweller, a statuesque creature, hair pinned high on her head, her face tilted slightly, listening—maybe to music, maybe to talk. She walks by and pays no heed to the woman crouching less than two metres from her.

Hunger finally propels me from my hideout. There's only one place I can go now, and I pray to every deity I can think of that I'm making the right decision.

I head south, towards the river and the bay. As I cross the main bridge and look out over the murk-brown river water, I feel exposed and giddy. I hurry past the casino on the other side, and the restaurants along the promenade, and jog through the quieter new housing district where the river opens out into docks and harbours.

I turn down the beach road and for a moment I am a fox, running, a red streak, as silver platoons swish past in all directions, flashing sunlight into my eyes so that I see white dots when I blink. Eventually I stop running, overwhelmed by thirst and the aching in my calves and the metal cutting into my wrists.

I can smell the sea now, and for an instant it conjures up the fresh, blue ocean of my childhood. But too soon, I am confronted by the slick, yellow-green bay. As I near the beach, the fall of the Dome's edge comes into view, like the backdrop of a giant stage, white and moonlike to the horizon.

I turn onto the boulevard alongside the beach. My father's home looms to my left—five floating pods above the original lower house, the maximum number that can be legally owned by one entity. He lives at the top. I stop, bend over, and catch my breath. I could stay curled up, scrabble back into my shell—anything to take me from the press of the sea on the one side and the opulent gravity of my father's estate on the other.

Instead, I stand up—for my daughter, for Gardner. My heart beats; a bird thrashing against a window in its last wild bid for freedom. But I do not count my heart, it is only half a heart now. Muscle and will alone are what get me to his door. I lift my manacled hands and press the buzzer.

An interface flickers to life against the wall and his face blooms in front of me. I'm shocked to see that his once dark hair has turned grey and his sun-browned face is now soft and pale. The eyes are the same though: shrewd and grave.

"Father."

"Anna?"

No expression registers on his face and I wonder what I'd expected. The door clicks open and I duck inside. The downward pull is strong on my stomach as the elevator rises up through the stem. Rooftops give way to the land laid out before me, a cityscape tinted green by the photosynthetic window glass.

He is waiting in the entranceway. As soon as he sees me, he turns and walks inside. I follow him across the threshold and the soft click of the door closing behind me is like a judge's hammer.

"Let me look at you," he says when we reach the living room. He steps back, his gaze travelling from my head to cuffed hands to my feet so that I feel like I'm standing at school assembly. "It's been too long, Anna, too long."

He gets me a glass of cold water and I gulp it down.

As he searches in another room for something to release me from my shackles, I take a place on his suede-soft couch, trying to be still so as not to dislodge too much of the dust and dirt from my clothes.

He returns with a bolt cutter.

"How's your mother?" The metal snaps.

It's not the question I'd expected.

"She's well. Healthy. She built a house. It's nice." I shrug. How to describe a world so far removed from this one?

"Why are you here Anna?"

"I need your help." He is silent. I'd rather face the Sphinx. "Freya has been taken from me. She's somewhere in the city. I don't know if she's alive."

"My granddaughter, whom I'm yet to meet." He shakes his head. "Lost her already? You never were very good at looking after your things."

I take a deep breath, try to still the rising blood so that I don't satisfy him with a retort. He watches the effect of his goading, analysing the depth and intensity of the sting.

"How can I help?"

"I need to stay here for a while."

He nods slowly. "That didn't work out very well last time, did it?"

"No, it didn't. I'm sorry. But I have nowhere else to go."

He stands up and collects my empty glass from beside me, holding it as though it's a chalice of sacramental wine.

"Let it not be said that I don't look after my own. You may stay. I'm afraid your old bedroom has been outfitted for other purposes, but you may use Fourth Pod. It is currently empty and fully furnished, with all the connectivity you will need to search for our Freya."

I release a breath. "Thank you." I get up and put my arms around him. He's taken aback I think, but he holds me briefly in the hug, and for that moment I can remember the love I had for this man. He still smells the same, of a subtle, aquatic cologne.

"Hobbs is delivering supper at seven," he says, straightening his suit. "Would you like to join me?"

My stomach betrays me with a loud gurgle.

IT'S BEEN SO LONG since I've thought of myself as the daughter of Charles Drake, CEO of Drake Industries and founder of the pioneering Photosyntech Corporation. We eat dinner in silence but I don't mind; it's a beautiful thing to be able to focus on the food laid out before me: a moist eye-fillet topped with a knob of melting butter, crisp roast potatoes and bright green beans. I try not to eat hurriedly but it is difficult; I've been hungry for so long. Hobbs pours a deep red wine into our glasses. I watch it swirl and settle and it looks like blood. Savouring food suddenly seems absurd.

My father takes a sip; his white lips are stained red. He brings a napkin to his mouth as if to wipe away the evidence of a crime.

"You are staring Anna. What is it? Is the meal not to your liking?"

I meet his gaze.

"It's delicious. Thank you."

"But you are thinking of your daughter."

I nod.

"Then why don't you tell me what this is all about, from the start, and then we will see what we can do."

I have no choice but to tell him about our journey across the New Desert, to relive the abduction of Gardner and Freya and to sketch, in the thinnest of detail, my encounter with and escape from Faulk Parker. I don't tell him everything, and I particularly avoid saying anything that would alarm him about Gardner; my mother and I decided long ago that it was best to keep that particular detail to ourselves.

He is watching me intently, scanning for any facial tic, change in the timbre of my voice or flicker of my gaze. He knows there are parts missing from my story, has always known that he has never had full access to my life. I don't lie to him though, not outright. To his employees he is 'The

Dragon', who'd burn a man to cinders should they dare to bring him an untruth. As far as I know, my father has never actually set anyone on fire, but his anger in the face of liars is something as wild and unpredictable. As the daughter of the dragon, I could always get away with partial truths, but learned early that direct lies would result in a scalding.

He leans back in his chair and clasps his hands together, one finger tapping minutely against the other, the only sign that he's not made of stone. He is silent as Hobbs sweeps in and clears away our plates. Then he asks the one question I don't want to answer, not yet.

"Why did you come to the city, Anna?"

"Because I need to find Freya and Gard—"

"No. Why were you coming here at all? I know how much you dislike it. How little you enjoyed your time here with me."

"I didn't dislike being with you."

"Answer the question." His voice has an edge now and his face is no longer pale. "Why are you here?"

I hesitate, my heart skipping up its tempo. All could be lost on one bead of words strung together the wrong way. There never really was a choice, though; right from the start, as far back as Freya's birth, I became beholden to her. I could not, would not change that.

"Freya. She...we were bringing her to the city. She has a rare condition that we need to see a specialist for. Someone who can help us learn more about it, to cure it if we can."

"Why didn't you contact me? I could have had you here in a few hours. I could have helped you with finances, a place to stay. Why traipse across the desert and put my granddaughter's life at risk?"

I look down at my hands.

"I'm sorry. I didn't want to burden you."

"Burden me?" His voice is rasping, as though his mouth is a box with the lid pressed so tight that it can only let out the barest of sound and I don't know if it's rage or some other emotion that he is pressing down upon.

"I'm sorry," I say again.

Hobbs enters the room, this time with dessert: sticky date pudding with custard and cream. Charles picks up his long, silver spoon.

"Eat Anna. You are as skinny as an alley cat."

9

FAULK

*I*n my dream, the sky is a purple bruise laid low upon me and the city hisses grey smoke into my ears. I am cracked and broken upon stones. They push and punch up underneath me, nagging me awake.

I open my eyes.

Pods, like ghostly half-ships sailing, pattern the sky. I try to read them as though they are words, sentences in white, all for me, all to tell me that I am lost, and she is gone.

The hissing comes again, and then I am moving upwards. It could be the end, or something new. The cat in my ears resolves to sound in a lower register and I realise that these are words, words that tell me I am a failed life. That I am lost and that Anna, my killer, is gone.

Goldengass, not God, is standing above me now.

"You useless pile of ballast."

That about sums it up. I'm pretending now, to be the unbreathing dead. Goldengass shakes me and I can no longer resist his vitriol.

I open my eyes again. Everything hurts. I cover my face

with my hands. You can't see me, so I mustn't be here. He slaps my face. Not very hard. Not compared with all the other pain.

I push up to sitting. Goldengass has red silk on today. Anything to direct the gaze of others away from his war-wounded legs.

"Nice pyjamas."

He reaches out for another slap, but I catch his wrist. It's stronger and harder than I would have imagined, like a pig's trotter. He pulls out of my grip and spits out words like wasted pips.

"A woman, a girl, and a dog. Why, Parker? When I gave you Mustenhause, you had him clocked, finished and buried within a day. The same with Christine C. So, it's not because she's a woman. It can't be that. Is it the girl? That she's a mother? I need to know Parker, or this is the last. I can't have this happen again, do you understand?"

"It's the last anyway." I say it before I fathom it. But it's true. It had once been like a golden gift, given to me by pain, born out of horror. But I was just a river, and that gold has washed through me, passed on, tumbled and gone. It was never mine. It was not a passion, not like with Goldengass.

He stares like he hasn't heard.

"You are my best."

"Then I am the worst of them."

Something catches in my ribs and I clutch at it.

Disdain is drawn all across his face, from his small, cold eyes to the soft droop of his mouth.

"Parker. There have only ever been two rules. One: you do what I ask, I make you rich. Two: there's no such thing as retirement." He waits, allowing the meaning to sink in. "Now, are you sure that this is your last?"

He isn't as pretty as my angel of death. I've always known

that reaper dude was bullshit; known that she's an angel like any other—softer, darker, maybe sweeter. I saw her that day in the rubble. She'd hovered over that sunken lot, gathering souls like corn, binding and holding them in her deep embrace; just another kind of mother.

I can't see her now, so I'm guessing Goldengass didn't come prepared; that it'll take him some small amount of time to get another one of us onto my case. So I figure I've got a few moments to change his mind.

"Let me find her."

He raises his eyebrows as though it's the funniest thing he's heard this week.

"I don't need her."

"Okay, maybe you don't, but she can still make trouble for you." He waits. It's not enough. "And you can take it as proof that I'm back in the game."

"And if you don't manage it?'

I shrug. "Retirement, I guess."

He smiles. "Parker, I love you like a son you know."

"Like the one currently fertilising your garden?"

"Yes, like that one."

I eat alone. He hasn't released me from his compound, but he's at least relieved me of his company. I swill and slug like it's the last feast, which, of course, it might be. The honey and peanut butter biscuits make me think of the traps my father used to make to catch the possums in our yard. Before the Retreat, when we lived on the outskirts, beyond the territory slated for inclusion in the Dome. He withstood the pressure for us to move for years, stubborn bastard, said he loved the trees, nothing and no one was gonna move him from his home to hide in town under some poncy doily.

In the end, Mum left, took us into the Dome. Mum didn't care about the trees, never had. She loved the glitz and glamour of city life. Didn't care about kids much either. We got in the way of her upscaled life. She tried not to bring the men home at first, more from embarrassment than any kind of loyalty to us. After we got our own pod, though, she worked hard to make it a place she could be proud of. That meant the kid stuff was consigned to one room, and we were shooed out whenever a gentleman caller came round. Kes and I spent those nights sleeping on the beach. From there, we could look up at the Dome roof and try to decipher the stars behind it. We told ourselves it wasn't even real darkness, tried to imagine we were safe. There was never anyone out there on the sand with us; all we ever heard was the quiet, lapping sea and the squawk and shift of sleeping seagulls. We made up stories to tell each other about what Dad was doing right now. Climbing up the old steel ladder to get those damn possums out of our roof. He'd be able to see the real sky from there. We had him climbing up all the way to upside-down Orion, cooking a meal for himself over Betelgeuse's bright red flame. Jumping on a fruit bat and flying home to us. He never did come to see us though. Before we were old enough to leave the Dome by ourselves, we got word he'd been burnt to a crisp trying to defend our home from a bushfire. Stubborn to the end.

Kes never let Mum forget. She stopped with the men, brought us back into the house, tried to bring us back into her arms. But we knew it was just to assuage her guilt, her renewed loneliness, knew it wasn't really about us. Kes left first, went off to become a teacher; guess he figured he could make some lives better, could give something to some strangers' kids that he never got himself. I admired him for it, but I couldn't understand it. The last thing I wanted to do was to go through childhood again and again.

I left a couple of months after. 'Soft military' was what

Kes called it. I started off wanting to be a hero. It was a new role in a security branch run by the private corporations involved in the Dome's maintenance. Dome Protection Officers began their training with the Federal Police but were syphoned off early to train for that alliance of companies in a more mercenary and eclectic style. It felt good and right and it gave me a structure and stability that my family had never provided for me. Goldengass was one of our trainers. He had me pegged back then for his own thriving side-business. He only had to wait for the right trigger. It was lucky for him then, when grief folded me in on myself like a cocoon. He made it his personal business to coax out just the kind of night-moth he was hoping for.

I look down at my plate. One sweet biscuit remains, one last piece of possum bait. I pick it up, breathe in the smell, breathe in my dad. Possum bait. I sit up straight. That's what I need to bring her out. Bait.

Goldengass is not quick to agree. There's something shifty around his eyes, something he's sitting on, like a dragon egg.

"Just the girl," he says finally.

"Sure." I shrug. Who else was there? The dog? Had he let it escape?

"You have half an hour."

I follow a guard through the warren of corridors and stairs that lead us ever downward to the cells. I've had no cause to visit them before; none of my previous targets were live captures.

As we wind deeper, I smell iron and damp. The light becomes softer and greener as we move from solar to photo-syn-enhanced fungi lining the walls like emergency strip-lighting. Finally, we stop at a metal door. The guard clicks it open and the door swings wide into a small room like a metal box.

I'm assaulted by the smell of ammonia. A tin bucket sits in one corner and, curled up amongst a few dank cushions in the other corner, is the girl. Her eyes are closed and her long fox-bronze hair lies across her cheek. She has her legs drawn up tight to her body, and her arms hugging them to her are still incongruously sun-browned.

I nod to the guard, and he withdraws. I hear the door click again behind him and push down a sudden panic of claustrophobia. Breathing deeply, I take out my bottle and pour some water into a cup that's sitting empty beside her. I bring up my interface and begin to take footage of her curled up there and sleeping. She opens her eyes, alert as a bird, and I realise she's only been feigning sleep.

Her gaze flickers from the cup of water to me and back to the cup. Then she snatches it up and guzzles until all the liquid is gone. She wipes the moisture from her chin with her hand, shuffles back against the wall, pulls a cushion to chest and stares hard at me without a word.

I can feel fight and fire in this slip of a girl, and I'm strangely glad of it. I didn't want to find a conquered child. Something releases inside me. Strength and steel I can deal with. I put my hand into my pocket and bring out a round, orange stone with a ring of ochre. I place it on the concrete floor between us. She looks down at it, then slowly reaches out and picks it up, her face a question. I nod.

"It's yours. You found it first."

She holds it to her like a talisman, brings its smoothness to her face, closes her eyes at the feel and smell of it. I start recording again. I don't need her to talk, just need her mother to know she's alive.

"What are you doing?" She is glaring.

"Sending a message to your mother. So she knows you're safe."

Her face softens into yearning, her eyes wide and deep with fear.

"Is Mummy all right?"

What do I say to her? *Actually, I clapped your mummy in irons. Then she kicked me in the balls, pickpocketed me and shot me with my own gun. Oh, and I'm tracking her down so I can hand her over to a scary old man who'll probably kill her.*

"She's very brave, your mum. She's going to be fine."

The kid is so young. The most fearful thing on her horizon should be starting school in a year or so. Goldengass was right; I'd lost the stomach for it. This was just sick. But it'd never been about real people before; always figures in the distance, caricatures of danger and harm. I'd still been playing hero, justifying every death as one more devil down, while Goldengass sat like a fat spider spinning a web full of lies for me to swallow like flies. Yeah right, poor innocent me. I've always known, not very far beneath the surface, the dubious nature of my deeds. But keeping a pre-schooler in a place like this, this was never the deal.

The guard returns. The girl hides her fearful baby eyes behind a shutter of stone and watches him like a cat on a wall.

"I've gotta go now."

She snaps to me with her stare. "Wait."

The guard looks at me. I shrug.

"Do you know where my daddy is?"

Didn't expect that one.

"No, I'm sorry."

She looks down at her hands.

I turn to go. "Catch ya later, kid."

"Will you come back?"

"Yeah, maybe, if you want?"

"I do."

"Okay then."

The guard pushes me out the door and closes it behind us. The click of the lock echoes in my head all the way up to the light.

"So how do we get it to her?"

Goldengass has got some lady giving him a haircut. He's mostly bald, so I could pretend I don't know why he's bothering, but she's something to appreciate, standing between Goldengass's legs with her bosom at his face. I turn away from the car crash to think before I answer.

"It has to be somewhere public, somewhere she's got access to. I'm betting she's still in the centre somewhere."

He lets me keep thinking out loud as the scissors snip and her hands smooth. When I've finally nutted it out, it feels like genius.

10

ANNA

I wake slowly from a silver dream. We're in a boat on a sea bright with sunlight. Freya, Gardner and I. The water shines and glints, angles into our eyes so that we can't see. Deep ocean fish rise to the surface all around us, then sink again. I look over the edge and can see one sailing downwards, slick like silk, into the inky deep. *Come back.* I reach and grab and lean too far; the boat tips and I am falling. The drop is long and I twist and turn to see Freya and Gardner silhouetted against the sky above me. *Mama!*

Freya's voice follows me into wakefulness. I open my eyes and sit up, my heart thudding. The room is white and bright. I get out of bed and walk across the skin-warm floor to the window. From Fourth Pod, I can see the foreshore laid out before me. The bay is pale green in the early light, the road already full of the swish and glint of platoons. A few people are jogging along the path by the beach. A group of rainbow lorikeets flashes past, their voices bright and rachety. I wonder what they think of their aviary; whether they ever wish they could fly up and out of the Dome.

The old trapped feeling arises within me. I turn away from the window to the desk against the wall and call up an interface. It wavers for a moment and then settles.

"Tracker ID list" I say. I already know it's a hopeless task, but I have to start somewhere. "Faulk Parker."

An image takes shape in front of me of a clean-shaven man, considerably less weathered and wearied than the one I met: with shorter and neater dark hair, smiling eyes— brownish, verging on green maybe; a nose that looks like it's been broken at some stage; knobbly and slightly askew. He's wearing a Dome Protection uniform: black with a white silk- moth logo. I read the bio below his photograph: *Occupation: Dome Protection Officer, Great Southern Dome; Training: Lochard Academy; Sex: Male; Age: 38; Next of Kin: Kes Parker, brother; Relationship: Widower; Status: Live.*

So, he survived. I breathe out some of the guilt. There's no address listed, but this is already more information than I'd expected. Of course, it could all be lies. But 'Widower'? I can't see why that'd be in there if it was all fabrication.

I'm trying to decide whether to start with the brother or the academy when there's a knock at my door. Hobbs arrives with breakfast on a tray. It's hidden under a silver lid, but I can smell bacon and it takes a lot of willpower not to jump on the food and gobble it up straight away. Hobbs places the tray on the table beside the window.

"Thank you."

He nods.

I watch him set down white plates and silver cutlery. He is old, slight and unsmiling. I don't remember him from my time with my father.

"Hobbs, is my father in?"

"No, he's not."

"Then perhaps you might be able to help me." He inclines

his head but shows no hint of emotion. I take this as consent. "I need some means of transport. My ID is inactive at present, so I can't take public transport."

"Of course, Ms Drake. Your father left instructions to aid you in any way you require. There is a vehicle at your disposal. Whenever you are ready, I can show you down to the garage."

"Great."

"Your father has also arranged a fitting for you this morning."

"A fitting?"

"You are to be provided with new clothes. A tailor will be in shortly to take your measurements."

"I'm sorry Hobbs, but I really need to get to town as soon as I can."

"Your father charged me with this particular detail and I would be loath to let him down."

I raise my eyebrows but say nothing. I don't want to place the man in an impossible situation. I console myself with the fact that I have some more research to do before I head out, anyway. Let the tailor come.

Hobbs leaves quietly, and I turn on my breakfast.

The tailor knocks on the door as I'm sipping my final dregs of coffee.

"Come in."

The door opens on a tall, squarish woman in a midnight blue suit with glimmer solar cells glittering all through it like stars. Her hair is white and pulled into a loose bun at the back of her head and her eyes are a pale ice blue, a strange contrast to the softness of her face.

"Hello dear, I'm Sirena, the tailor. Are you ready?"

Her movements are efficient and practiced as she holds up a little bronze box that beeps at my head and then at my toes, at my waist, bust and hips. She holds it against my hair and then brings it up next to my face. Her long fingernails click against buttons and more beeps issue from the box until at last she nods.

"I'm going to get this printed for you. Then I'll come back and we can do some fine-tuning. All right?"

For the first few minutes after she's gone I find myself wandering around the apartment like a trapped fly. Eventually, I pour myself some water, plunk down on the soft white couch and pull up the next item in my search: *Women's Hospital Bombing.* I scan the article, wondering why this came up. Did Faulk Parker have something to do with this act of violence? At the end is a list of victims. There are hundreds. I'm less than a quarter of the way through their histories when Sirena returns.

She holds up a dark green outfit that looks like a dress over leggings, though it's all one piece, spangled with glimmer solar cells and has the strangest trim at the neck and hem: something filamentous, curved into a shell-like lattice, with an organic, sculptural life of its own.

I must look wary because Sirena drops her voice like she's shushing a nervous horse.

"Give it a go, you'll find it's a lot more comfortable than it looks."

"How do you even get into it?"

She turns it around, opens it up and holds it out for me to step into.

"Here, I'll help you balance."

I clutch her shoulder as I step into the suit and she joggles it up around me and fastens it with a quicksilver zip up my side.

"There. How does it feel?"

I swish around a bit and look down to see the latticework falling into a subtler relief against the swinging folds than I had expected.

"Comfortable, actually."

"Good." She grabs my arm and leads me to the full-length mirror. "Here, put these on." She hands me a pair of green silk slippers. I take them. They are light and I turn them over to see tough-looking running soles. I pull them on without argument. "There!" She moves me back so that I can see the full length of my outfit. "What do you think?"

It looks strange to me, but I can appreciate a kind of eerie beauty in the effect. She's playing with my hair now, brushing it and pulling it up into braids.

"This is the latest style in the Southern Domes."

We both appraise the stranger in the mirror. I look like a Dome citizen now, which is all that matters.

Sirena adjusts one last braid.

"There, don't you look a treat?"

The next moment, she is smiling and hugging me at the door. I feel a rush of something like gratitude as I watch her step into the lift. Then it's my mother out there in her new cave house who is in my mind, and my missing her is like a bellyache.

Hobbs leads me to the vehicle downstairs. He runs me through its programming instructions and closes the door after me as I settle into the seat. I choose my destination as the Library, near the Square, the last warehouse for the city's pre-digital records. The address I'm looking for is not available on-line. Gardner knew it, but Gardner isn't here.

The car stops below the Square, in one of the few carparks that hasn't been converted to housing. As most people travel by platoon, owning a private car is an exorbitant luxury, unaffordable to the majority. I don't want to attract attention, so an underground carpark and a walk down the main street suits me well.

I emerge, squinting, into the bright city. No one stares this time; I'm just one amongst a multitude now. I take my first breath of freedom since leaving the desert. In this disguise, I can do anything. For a moment, I am strong and optimistic that they are alive and that I will find them.

I EMERGE FROM THE LIBRARY, triumphant. I'd been the only one there, and the bored officials had seemed pleased to have had something to do. I tuck the address into the pocket in a fold of my outfit and begin the walk back along the Main Street bridge.

Looking down from the bridge onto the river, I see it's still brown, despite all the efforts to return it to clarity. During Construction they re-planted river red gums along-side the water and re-introduced platypus. The trees have grown now, strong and shady, but I can almost hear the river's spite, its murking and frothing at the city that forced itself upon her banks.

I turn from the river, and with her at my back, trudge uphill towards the carpark and the Square.

"What are you doing?"

I spin around, my heart a racehorse in my chest. *My girl!* I am disorientated, distraught as I scan the city crowd for Freya.

"Is Mummy all right?"

This time I see her. The massive black screen above the Square flickers to life and there she is; sitting up, hugging a filthy cushion to her as though it's a doll.

"What are you doing?"

"Is Mummy all right?"

The reel plays and replays. My daughter's face, stern and wary. *My daughter. Alive!*

I am crying. I am kneeling on the pavement and I am crying.

"Are you all right?"

A woman is crouching next to me. She puts her hand against my back. I nod.

"Yes…I just…fell over."

"Anything broken?"

"I don't think so." She helps me stand and guides me to a shelf of concrete so I can sit down.

"Here, I just bought this tea, haven't drunk it yet, you can have it, it'll help with the shock."

She brings it to my lips. Before I can think, a warm, sweet liquid is entering my mouth. I swallow.

"Just rest." She holds my arm to steady me. Which is good because the world is swirling in a blur of colour and sound. "Here—have another sip." I only just swallow before the world turns gold and I fall into a black hole.

11

FAULK

*T*he hairdresser calls. It has all happened so much more quickly than I'd expected. I tell her to wait with her.

When I get there, Anna is out cold and the hairdresser is vacant with boredom.

"Forgot your glasses?"

"About time! Here, hand me yours; my VR-cast's started."

I hand her my headset. "You've got ten minutes."

"It'll be over in five." She switches on and her eyes switch off. I get her to help me haul Anna to my waiting car and the hairdresser moves like an automaton, as removed from me as the unconscious woman we are laying out across the seat.

We pile in and the car starts to move. Anna's head is on my lap. I look down at her sleeping face, her smooth, brown skin, the sparse arch of freckles across her nose, and lips that curve like small smiles at the edges. I touch my hand to her intricate braids. I want to touch her cheek, but I don't.

"Okay." I reach for the headset. The hairdresser puts up a manicured forefinger. One more minute.

The car lurches to a stop and I only just stop Anna falling.

"Hey!" The hairdresser looks around at me in outrage. "Who stopped the cast?"

"It's not just the cast."

"What? Why aren't we moving?"

I open the door manually to the silver honk of a platoon behind me.

"Come on, out! I need to take a look." She huffs onto the pavement and I get in the front, push a few buttons, tweak a few dials but it's dead, no power. Platoons overtake our car and the traffic flows around us as though we're a rock in a river. "Give me the glasses." She hands them back. I try to call up an interface but nothing happens. "Help me get her out again, we've gotta get her back before the drug wears off."

The hairdresser is irritated. She drops Anna's legs to the pavement. I scowl at her.

"Well, she's heavy!"

I bring Anna's limp arm around my neck like the day we met and haul her back to the raised grass verge. It's as I let go of her wrist that I feel it: a small square in the fabric. I turn the sleeve inside out.

"What are you doing?"

"It's a heart tracker. Must've sent out a death pulse when it worked out she'd been drugged. That's why we lost power."

"Great."

I rip it out of the fabric.

"Does that mean someone's coming for her?"

"I don't know."

The hairdresser puts her hand on her hips. "Well, I'm not sticking around to find out."

She steps into the path of a platoon, which brakes to a stop. I watch her peer in the windows of the first few cars until she finds one that's empty. Then she climbs in and it takes off again.

I look down at my prisoner, so peaceful on the grass.

"Why'd you have to make it so hard?"

Her breathing flutters. I bend down and scoop my arms beneath her.

"Come on, let's get you somewhere before someone comes calling."

12

ANNA

I open my eyes and for a moment I can see only white. It resolves into a pale sky. I am strung out in the air, looking out over nothing.

I try to orient myself in this white upon white, light upon light world. A dark shape is growing larger, no, coming closer: black, upswept wings, tail like a diamond: a wedge-tailed eagle soaring towards me. It swoops so close that I can see the gold in its feathers; then it lifts over and away. I gasp and sit up to catch a last glimpse as it disappears above me.

"Lost her mate last year. Used to be a family but the chicks have all grown up and left."

Faulk Parker is standing at the doorway on the other side of the room, holding a glass of water. He is more recognisable from his photograph without the desert dust.

I am sitting on a divan by a floor-to-ceiling window. Faulk sets the glass down on a table next to me.

"For you." He winces as he lowers himself into a chair.

"And why would I drink anything you've got to give me?"

He shrugs. "Because you're thirsty."

I pick up the glass, bring it to my lips. The water is fresh and cold and I want more. "I didn't kill you then."

"Appears not."

"Where's my daughter?"

"Straight to the point."

"Where is she?"

"Alive."

"Where?"

"Won't be long before you can see her."

"Is Gardner with her?"

"The dog?"

"Yes, the dog."

"Not sure where your mutt ended up, to be honest. You can find out for yourself soon enough."

"You really don't know what you're involved in, do you?"

He shakes his head, smiling. "Nope, just doing my job."

"And you're experiencing high job satisfaction right now? Holding minors against their will, separating and terrorising families?"

"From what I hear, Ms Drake, you lot are the terrorists."

"You are so off base."

He gets up. "I'm going to get us some food. Make yourself at home."

"Where are we?"

"My place. Keep an eye out for the eagle, she might come back."

He closes the door.

I'm not shackled so I'm guessing he's confident there's no easy escape route. I get up to test my feet. I'm steady enough but feel dull and achy, and my bladder is full. I discover the bathroom and sit with a disconcerting view over the clouds; the room is huge and airy and the washbasin is big enough to bathe a child in. I splash cold water over my face again and again, and the braided creature in the mirror drips back at me. I bury my face into the towel. Its softness brings me to Freya and my mother and Gardner all at once, and to missing their touch to aching.

When I go back into the room, he's already there with a tray of food. I want to shake him and cry and pummel him. But I say nothing and eat his food because it will give me the strength to fight him. And I *will* fight him, in whatever way I can, until I have my family back with me. And then I will fight whoever is above him, pulling the strings of their marionette.

"So, tell me then."

He'd been silent for so long I'd almost convinced myself I was alone. I look up from my food.

"Tell you what?"

"What it is I'm involved in."

I take another sip of water. It's my turn to appraise him. He takes it, unflinching. There's a shadow in his face. The lost eagle, perhaps.

"First tell me about your wife."

"I don't have one."

"You had one."

It's the hunted animal's instinct that tells me to be still and silent; to watch and wait. I lock onto his gaze and the struggle plays out in the space between us. I don't back down until the silence shifts, vibrates with the bargain we strike in its unfolding waves: I'll tell you; you tell me.

"Her name was Mia."

"What happened?" I ask, even though I think I know.

"We had a child. The Women's Hospital Bombing. He was born the night before." I wait for him to continue. He takes a deep breath. "I'd gone home to get fresh clothes, bring her some decent food. Came back and they were gone."

He isn't looking at me anymore, he's staring into the sky. The silence is heavy, my fight almost gone.

"So why are you doing this?"

He turns back to me.

"You mean, where's all the love gone?" There's a hardness in his eyes. "There's nothing good here, Ms Drake. Not anymore. Now you tell me. Why does Goldengass want you and your daughter?"

"Goldengass?"

"My boss. My turn. What's the deal?"

"I don't know."

"Come on, you can do better than that."

"All right. Freya—my daughter. She's different. She's got a condition I can only imagine must be of some sort of interest to your boss."

"A condition?"

"An ability really."

"So she's some kind of prodigy?"

I shake my head. "No, not exactly. It's hard to describe."

He tries a different tack.

"Why were you on your way to the city?"

"To visit a specialist who knows about her condition."

"Who?"

"I can't tell you that."

"You can tell me or tell my boss."

"I'll be telling him anyway, apparently."

"That depends."

"On what?"

"On how good your answers are."

The light in the room fades as a dark shape looms again. I turn to watch her through the window. She barely flaps. She's so close I can see each feather finger vibrating against the updraft.

A soft chime sounds from somewhere in the pod and she soars away. Faulk gets up, suddenly tense and wary.

"Wait here."

As if I could go anywhere else.

After a moment, he returns to stand in the doorway.

"I've gotta run an errand. There's no way out, so don't bother trying. If you're hungry, there's food in the kitchen." He pokes his thumb over his shoulder to a door behind him. "Help yourself."

Then he's gone.

I get up and move around, stretch my legs back into action and walk the curved edges of the room. On a silver tray upon a table along the wall is a bottle of something clear. I turn the label outward: gin. Next to it are several small glass vials, each a different colour. I pick up a rose pink one and read the label: 'Joy'. Then a red one: 'Sex' and a green one: 'Nature'. I unscrew the lid of the last one and sniff it. A hot tang of eucalyptus oil shoots up my nose. I manage to place the vial back on the tray before I turn, staggering to the lounge behind me. Green leaves rain from a golden sky. And there she is, looking down at me, her hair a wild mane, skin shining like a chestnut.

"Shama!" My voice is a loud whisper, echoing around a silent forest. I reach my arms to her, my body thrumming with wildness and longing. "I've missed you so much." She smiles and takes my hands, pulls me into a fierce whirl of leaves and fire and rain. I take it all into me, soak in it, drink it up with a thirst I'd forgotten I had.

We run, and bushes claw and tangle. We run so fast. Run and fall into water. I swirl and turn like a whirligig beetle, laugh out bubbles, watch them rise silver to the surface. She has my hand and we platypus paddle in and under dark red gum roots like caves, burst up beneath hanging lianas. The air is spiced with nutmeg and camphor and deep, sweet mulch. I fall back onto a bed of moss, breathing it in, my eyes gold-bright with sunlight. There are warm stones on the palms of my hands. Their heat seeps through me, softening away the cold, stored up places, heating me through.

"Shama, what have I forgotten?"

She strokes my hair, tender as a mother. *"Nothing. Just don't forget to remember."*

"And it's still here?" My voice echoes as though I've called into a chasm.

"Always."

Always.

I'm falling now. Falling up and away from her. I land with a jolt and open my eyes. The room is dark, my tongue, stuck and dry. I swallow to bring some saliva to my mouth and try to stand. Everything spins. I stagger to the window and kneel on the divan. Outside is dark blue, and beyond the Dome roof the stars are strung like jewels across the sky.

I sit with my knees curled up to my chin and look out onto the world. My heart is so full of yearning and loss that I'm afraid if I move, I will burst with it.

There's no sound in the pod, no hint of movement to suggest that Faulk Parker is here. I'm glad. I need to rest. I lie down, pull the throw rug from the back of the divan over me, and close my eyes.

13

FAULK

*G*oldengass is getting edgy. He's summoned me to his compound. We're in the velvet room. The red velvet covering the entire floor and curved walls is like a bloody womb. The orange glow of the lamps only adds to the impression that you're up against skin, trapped in a place of floating and waiting.

Goldengass is reading beneath one of these lamps as I enter.

"Where's my hairdresser, Parker?"

I'm surprised. I thought she'd raised the alarm on me. It gives me an unexpected advantage. I wonder what she's playing at. Did she see it as her chance to bolt? To leave the employ of her flesh-grabbing boss. Maybe she really did fancy herself as a hairdresser.

"I dunno."

Goldengass narrows his already narrow eyes.

"And how are you progressing?"

"All going to plan so far."

"Parker, you may be a killer, but you're a lousy bullshit artist. Where's Anna?"

"I know where she is. Got her pinned. Just need to retrieve her, so how about you let me get on with my job."

He gives me another stony stare and then returns to his book. With a flick of the wrist, I'm dismissed.

I walk into the courtyard as the watering system finishes up and the place becomes peaceful. A solitary cricket chirrups in the damp grass. Water trickles into a small pond. I dig into the quiet for the sound of voices or footsteps from inside. Nothing.

I cross the courtyard and enter the building on the other side. The fungi-lit exit lines are bright enough that I don't need to turn on any lights. I find the stairwell and begin the descent. It's quiet down here too. Few prisoners. Perhaps only the one.

I find Freya's cell again with little trouble and push open the slot, quietly so as not to wake her in case she's sleeping. In the green gloom, I see her start and sit up. Obviously not quiet enough.

"It's just me. Sorry to wake you up."

"I wasn't asleep."

"Here, brought these for you."

I place an apple and a biscuit on the narrow frame of the slot and hold the metal open until I hear the scrape of her feet and see her little hands grabbing them from the ledge. Then I take a kids' picture book from inside my coat pocket and angle it through the slot; it only just fits.

"What's this?" Her voice is a loud whisper.

"Used to be mine. Before that, it was my dad's. It's an old story: *The Little Engine that Could*. Thought you might like it."

"Thanks."

"Hey, your mum's alive and well."

"What? How do you know? Have you seen her? Is she worried about me?"

"Yes, and yes. But I'll tell her you're okay so she doesn't worry so much."

"But I'm not okay."

I don't know what to say to that one.

"I want to see her."

"And she wants to see you too. You'll get to soon."

She is silent. I look in to see she's back amongst the pile of cushions, clutching the book.

When she speaks, I can hardly hear her.

"Do you promise?"

I try not to hesitate.

"Yes. I promise. Try and get some shut-eye now, all right?"

"Okay."

I creep back up the stairs. *What are you doing, Parker?* The voice is so loud in my head it feels like it's come from somewhere outside me. I think I can smell her—violets all over a grave; my patient, reaping angel. Only a girl in a field collecting wildflowers, dealing death in summer.

I ENTER MY POD. It's dark and quiet and Anna is sleeping. I open the door to her room. The moon has risen, and it's shining on her. She looks peaceful; her face unlined and pale as wax under its light.

This was not the deal. I shake my head into the darkness. This was never the deal.

I go to my bed and dream in calligraphy. Black and swirling like words for me to read, as though there's a way through for me, a way home. I shot a devil in the back once and she fell like paper. Only she wasn't a devil. I made her so. I can't even remember her face. But why would I want to? Goldengass's pasty hands are clean and mine run red. From shadow to shadow, dawn to dawn, they dance for me: my charcoal ghosts.

I startle awake. It's late, and she's gone, I know it. She's no longer by the window. Without even grabbing on a shirt, I race around the apartment, panic washing through me.

I find her in the kitchen, boiling eggs.

For a moment I mistake her. She is my wife, ready to turn and smile. And then I feel the very wrongness of it all and I'm overcome with a staggering bitterness and I hate her; hate her more than she must hate me, her dithering jailer.

She speaks but doesn't turn around.

"There's one for you."

She drains the water, and steam rises around her as though she's already an apparition. She tips the eggs onto a plate and watches them spin to a stop. Then she sits at the kitchen table, holds one in a tea towel and picks away the shell. There's surrender in her stillness, fight in her eyes.

She reaches for the second egg and starts on that one too. She's like a magnet. I can't stop looking at her.

"Coffee?" I ask, only to break the spell.

She shrugs. "Sure."

I clatter around loudly enough to fill the quiet and put my stamp back on the kitchen. She watches me with that same cat-look as her daughter. Finally, I place a mug of black liquid in front of her and pull up the other chair. She takes a sip, and another, daring me to be the first to speak. I don't. Silence yawns between us.

She begins it almost absentmindedly and then more deliberately—slowly, slowly, she starts to unplait her braids. Bronze, twisted strands flick free against her skin. I breathe in the citrus release of shampoo and watch until her hair is long and full against her body. She doesn't flinch from my gaze.

I get up. Stop her fingers in their unweaving and pull her to standing. I bring her hands to my chest, place her palms over the two round burns.

"I did that?" She doesn't sound apologetic, only curious.

I nod, draw her closer. She will burn me. But there is the smooth plane of her cheeks, and her lips, dry and pink from the sun, her brown collar bone, and the smell of her: all salt and desert, and such heat rising through me I can't let her go.

She slides her hands slowly downwards, leaving trails of fire across my skin. Her fingers stop below my navel. I take hold of her wrists. She is a wild creature contained by my grip, pulsing with heat and fierceness.

She raises her chin and her clear eyes hold mine. "Will you take me to my daughter?"

I hate only myself as I press her to the floor and breathe a *yes* into her breast.

14

FAULK

I walk into the day. The Dome-muted sunlight is too bright. I need darkness, I need cover. If I was once a man, what am I now? More man or less? The species that ties their good, their promises, to reward. Like a dog. No better and so much worse. I was never the one who tore the wings from flies to watch them spin. But I watched the others do it. And look—how well I knew what to do when the time came.

I walk to think, walk to act because that is what I am, a man of action. And wasn't it fine, my action? Didn't her body smell like the sea, feel like a deep pool to drown in, a deep fucking drink of the divine. I find I can't regret it. If it makes me evil, then so be it. That is what I am.

And so then to the promise. If I can take what I want, what's a promise but a weakness? And I can choose to be weak, or not.

Only I can't go back to her accusing face, or worse, her hopeful eyes. *Take me to my daughter*, that's what she asked, what I promised. That I can do. Make it Goldengass's problem. And that way I get to live. A bonus, to be sure.

I walk along the foreshore, the sad sea lapping at the abandoned yellow beach. I am the only one under the seagulls. One bad man, no one to see him or know him. Kes got all the sweetness. Being younger, he was less easy to disappoint. He couldn't remember the way it once was. When our mother smiled and wanted us in her arms, when our father was just a rascal, not a hard, stubborn bastard.

A wind whips up the sand, blows granules in my face. I hope for a storm, a big busting super-storm to wash at me and wring me out. Something to hurt me and be my anger and my pain. Darkness swells in quick-building clouds, cumulonimbus giants with fists raised to thrash and tear at the city of writhing pupae beneath its silk. But it never rains here, not the real stuff. I look up at the Dome roof. The clouds disgorge and a tempest tantrums around it. The sky is silver with rain-splash and I'm at the bottom of a pool looking up towards a surface roughened by wind and water. They will collect the rain. It'll run into rivers and pipes to be saved up for a scheduled rainfall event. But not a drop will fall on me today. Today, I am given nothing.

The air is electric, as though all that holding back power has given it a charge. I can feel something rising within me, something like strength; something that tells me to get back there and finish it now. Be done with this assignment. Hand over the toy, she's not yours to play with anymore. I don't even have to see her again. Goldengass knows where I live.

Before I make the call, there's one promise I make to myself. I am not going back to him.

I walk to a chemist, buy some antiseptic, a bandage and some forceps. My pocket knife will be good enough to do the job. I return to the beach to be alone, sit with my back against the retaining wall and wipe my knife clean. I'm lucky I can pinpoint the precise location; there's a small scar in my thigh where they injected it at birth and I just hope it hasn't travelled too far since. I dig the blade into my flesh. The pain is far greater than I'd expected and I double over with nausea. Breathing to steady myself, I stuff the bandage into my mouth and bite down. I cut in again, one more time. It's not deep, just under the skin a little further south of the scar. I pull out the small square of metal: my tracker ID. Now I'm like her, a Dome citizen no more. I wrap the bandage tightly around the streaming wound. I'm dizzy as I stand and limp to the water's edge, but I want to do it quickly. I throw the tracker into the sea and I can almost hear it fizz and die in the salt and acid.

DESPITE MY CONVICTION, I can't resist seeing Anna one last time. Just the idea of it is like a drug juicing up my blood. I won't go home, but I can watch. Then, when they're gone, I'll make a last visit inside, pack a few essentials and lock up before I go off-grid. The pain in my leg has eased enough that I can walk on it and by the time I'm nearing my pod tree I'm almost running, high with the prospect of escape. I'm trading her freedom for mine. Fair trade. I try not to think of her daughter in a cell. Instead, I remember Anna's long, strong legs, the smell of her salt and the sweetness of her mouth.

I find my place beneath an old jacaranda, spreading and heavy with purple flowers. The shadow beneath it is deep and the view towards the entrance is clear. Once I make the call, it won't take Goldengass long to pick her up. I lean against the knobbled old tree-trunk and check that the headset is still working after my repairs. I'm about to call when I see a private car pull up and two men in trooper gear climb out. They buzz in and disappear through the main doorway.

It doesn't take me long to dismiss the idea that Golden-gass already knows and has come to fetch her; this team is different, they're in dark blue instead of black, with no silk-moth logo. When they come back out again, she is with them. Her hair is wet, as though the rain found only her, and solemn and straight between them. I find myself looking for the fight in her eyes, but I'm not close enough to see.

Proud Margaret stood in her father's doorway, straight as a willow wand. A folk song my grandmother used to sing me to sleep with, rises from the depths. I can hear her warbling voice in the dark. *Along there came the gardener bold; a red rose in his hand. I shall make a cloak for you out of the summer flowers.* But she made a cape for him instead, out of the winter snow and showers, and told him: *I wish you were away, away. I wish you were away.*

So, there she stands, not my Anna at all; never mine. It was love that brought her into my over-willing arms, but not love for me.

I, who once had a child but was never a parent, I can walk away. There's no pull for me, nothing that will bring me again and again onto the harder road. I can walk away. I watch until they're gone.

As I re-enter the silent apartment with my empty things waiting for me, I envy the ties she has to this world, the bright white threads that bind her. Because she can feel passion, not just the empty cavity of loss and the mud-grey pap that fills it up and calls itself my life.

I'M HEADING DOWNRIVER when I first get the feeling. It's a heat on the side of my face—someone watching me. The river banks are lush with sword-grass and fallen red gum branches. I'm scrambling up and over and through the dense vegetation. Eventually I give up and follow a wombat trail back to the main path, my idea of keeping out of sight defeated by the crashing sounds I make trying to move through the re-vegetated bush.

There are a few people out on health breaks, taking walks by the rolling swell of the water, but I can't see anyone particularly turned my way. The old fig trees squawk with fruit bats as I walk by one of their camps.

I'm headed for River Mouth exit. Anyone can pass out that way without a tracker ID. They just can't get back in. My plan is to stick along the coastline. I figure there'll be more forage there and that the sea will temper the heat. I can swim in creeks when I need to keep cool or get clean.

My leg is throbbing at the wound site and I find a spot in the shade to re-apply some antiseptic. As I'm dabbing, I feel it again. I look around me, stare hard into the shadows. If one of Goldengass's crew has clocked me, why are they taking so long?

I listen. Not a breath, not a rustle.

A kid whizzes by on a hover scooter, his long hair streaming, and a sleepy magpie starts up a warble from a branch above me. I get up, shrug on my backpack and get back to walking.

The path eventually leaves the city trees and opens out into a wetland. On either side is the old industrial zone, now converted to new housing. Pods float above their white reflections in an expanse of water crammed full of water-birds. I stop to watch a group of pelicans perched on a sand spit. They lift their long wings and jibe at each other with their gullety bills. I wonder if they know they're the chosen few, whether they ever think of their wild cousins. Drips of sweat roll down the side of my face out here on the bridge. The Dome has made me soft; a blind, white fish in a cave pool. Time to get back out there. Into the dust and dry.

I step off the bridge and into a stand of paperbark trees. Their flaky, flesh-toned trunks rise straight out of the water. The low sun sends ripple-light sparkling into my eyes, etching onto my retinas, blinding me to the path ahead. That's when it appears. I see it with that snow across my eyes, in the confounding light and shade of the thicket: a sandy dog; a dingo, sitting on its haunches in the middle of the path, staring me down.

I saw it only from a distance during those red dust days, but I know this is the one. Something about it prickles my skin. I stop still and breathe. The only thing you can control, the breath. Some of my old training kicks back in under threat. And there is such threat in its eyes.

I lift my hands slowly in front of me. *Look, nothing here to hurt you, dog.* It lowers its head in a flat growl and bares its teeth. That's enough for me; I take off my backpack, swing it around and shout.

"Come on, mutt! Try it on!"

It leaps at me in a great, springing bound and I am slammed to the ground, winded, its great front paws pinning me down, clawing into my chest, yellow teeth and hot breath up in my face. I squeeze my eyes shut. I can hear its great wet nose drawing in the scent of me and I shrink inwards, preparing for the bite. But it doesn't come. Instead, a pained howl bells into my ears and the pressure is released. I open my eyes and scramble to stand. It's already far away. I watch it bound from the path and ghost off into the thicket.

I stagger and fall back, relief fuzzing through me, making

me weak. Sitting and shivering, allowing the adrenalin to wash through, I strain to hear through the living silence: fish plopping for bugs at the water's surface and the crack and shift of the trees all around me. But there's no sound of the dog.

Eventually, cool air funnelling off the lake reminds me it's late in the day and that I need to get moving. I travel quickly and quietly, alert to the smallest cues around me. It won't catch me off guard again.

By the time I've walked another half hour, I've made my decision. I won't reach River Mouth by sundown and I need to rest. I find a relatively sheltered spot and eat some food, listening out for any signs of the mutt. There's nothing. I wait awake for a couple more hours, listening in the darkness just to be sure, before allowing myself, finally, to doze off. I tell myself it's only for a few hours, that I'll be on my way again well before sunrise.

15

ANNA

*F*aulk has gone. I don't know where. I can still feel the cold at my back from the kitchen floor, the novelty of his body, his heat and wetness, and for once I'm grateful for my fitful moon cycles since Freya's birth.

Gardner. Where are you? The man in him might forgive my motivation, but I cannot help but think that I've thrown a great darkness over us. All I can see out the window is blue. Forget-me-not blue.

It seems a just punishment that Freya's milk, my last comfort and body memory of her, has run dry. Oh Freya. I hold her name like a talisman as I go to the shower to wash myself clean.

I'm attempting to re-braid my hair when I hear the doorbell. He must be back, maybe with Freya. I pull on my shoes and run to the door. The chime comes again and I realise that of course it's not Faulk; he wouldn't ring to enter his own home. The door is locked from inside. I try to see through the frosted panelling.

"Stand back!"

I reel backwards as the door comes shattering down.

"Ms Drake!" Two men with helmets and batons are standing on the threshold. I freeze. It's too late to flee. "Ready to come home?"

Home. My mother's arms beneath an open sky. I am more than ready. But that is not the home he means.

"I..." My daughter, so near. I look around with the wild calculation of an antelope. Here is a lion; another is somewhere behind. "I need one more day."

"Our orders were very specific. Any deviation will require direct negotiation with your father."

They step either side of me and I see myself reflected in their black visors, no different to Freya and Gardner on the hill.

"Yes. Of course."

They grip my arms and guide me out.

WHEN WE ARRIVE, my father is not there. The guards leave me only once they're sure I'm ensconced in Fourth Pod with all the doors locked. I'm informed they'll be keeping watch at the main entrance. And so, I retire to my second well-furnished jail for the day.

Wasting no time, I pull up an interface and search for 'Goldengass'.

Thalas Goldengass, Senior Dome Protection.

There is nothing else. No personal details, no address, no history. The profile of a powerful man.

I get up, needing to hit something, to tear something. I'd been so close, given so much to be that close.

In the bathroom, I splash water on my face. I will speak to my father tonight. I have to get back to Faulk Parker. I look in the mirror and a trapped thing looks back at me—a woman surrounded by men like iron bars, with no key, no way out, save by their mercy and favours. When did it come to this? My proud, free mother, growing ferns in the desert dust; how did she defy it all so that she could live in freedom? I have her strength in my body, her grit in my veins. Yet here I am.

I look for it in my own eyes, for that which I know is mine. Time has lent me nothing but the need to be stronger, wilder, wilier. It is for them that I search—for Freya and Gardner—but it is also for me.

Hobbs brings food.

"Is my father in?"

"No, he's away on business until the end of the week."

My anger flares, but I breathe until I can speak calmly.

"I need a car again tonight."

"With respect Ms Drake, your father has asked that you remain here until he returns."

"I see. Thank you, Hobbs."

I close the door.

I eat because it is necessary. I will sleep tonight because my body demands it. But I will not stay here.

In the morning, the rising sun is hidden behind two veils, the Dome roof and white clouds to the horizon. I dress and re-braid my hair. The result is passable; enough not to draw attention.

Attention.

It only now occurs to me—how did my father find me? I'm struck by my stupidity. I pull off my clothes and lay the outfit out on the bed so that I can run my hands along its seams. I find a torn part inside the sleeve that I hadn't noticed before, but I am looking for something else. There is nothing. I feel across the fabric for a lump, a bump, anything.

97

Eventually I give up, confounded. It's only as I'm dressing again that I find it—a small square of metal tucked in at the base of the zip. I take to it with scissors. It leaves a small hole, but I'm elated. I put the tracker in the back of the desk drawer. Let them think that I'm spending my time sitting here, waiting for my father.

I pack some scraps of food saved from last night's meal, some bread, fruit and packaged oddments I find in the kitchen, an old jar that I fill with drinking water and a towel that I can use as a pillow or to keep me warm and dry should I need it. Lastly, I slip a folded piece of paper into the side pocket; Faulk's home address. I've studied the map and figure it'll take me about an hour to walk there. Short work to get me closer to my daughter.

My trip down the stem is unimpeded. I look out over the green-tinted city. We're off to see the wizard. I can see so much more in this uniform cloud-light. The town is below me. It is all a game. Some pieces are still, some are moving, but all are in flow. From here I can see, as if I've borrowed the eye of fate for a moment's glimpse. *Now. Do it now.* I feel into the heart of the Dome, burrow my mind like a grub into the space and time of it, for her, for my daughter, until I can feel a thread; moon-bright, from the hollow inside of me to her beating heart. And I know which way I must travel. Another thread, like a bridge, shoots out, away from her, towards a flat shimmer of silver and green. Is it Faulk? Gardner? I can't tell. Their essences are entangled and my body's response is only heat and fear.

By the time the lift door opens, my vision has dissipated and I am drained and shivering. There is only one guard. He sees me and rises to standing. I stagger to a seat in the lobby.

"Are you all right, Ms Drake?" He walks over, lifts his

visor. He's just a young man with a worried face. "You look ill. I'm going to call my supervisor."

He brings his hand up to his headset and, in doing so, reveals a weapon at his waist, only centimetres away from me. I have it out of its holster and up against his throat before he can talk.

"Don't move," I whisper into his ear.

I reach around, lift off his headset, throw it onto the ground and crush it with my foot until I hear something crack inside it.

A muscle twitch in his arm warns me he's about to try something. I dig the weapon further into his skin. "I *will* use this." I kick the headset away. "Let me leave and we'll have no trouble between us. Yes?"

"Yes." His voice is hoarse with fear.

I lift the weapon away slowly and point it at him as I back out of the door.

Then I turn and run towards the wetland. It's only when I reach a dense thicket of paperbarks and tea tree around the other side of the lake that I allow myself to stop. I can't see or hear anyone behind me. My heart is burning and my calves are stiff and cramped. I stumble off the track and double over, clutching at a tree stem as I gasp for air.

It takes a few moments to get my breath back. Having the gun in my hand feels like grasping a venomous snake. I toss it into the water. It lands with a satisfying plop.

I begin to follow something—a scent, a trail, a memory of the silver thread. It turns in my gut and guides me. If I try to think, to make it a more conscious thing, it slips from me. It's something below my senses; not smell or heat or cold or colour, yet almost all of these; it is a feeling that I follow and it leads me alongside the mud-fringed lake. A kingfisher flashes blue in the corner of my eye and flies ahead of me.

Follow me. It doesn't speak, but I hear it, and I walk along its quick, flapping line. It's an azure dart in the morning gloom. Stop. Wait. Zip. Then, as suddenly as it appeared, it leaves me, shooting low across the water and out of sight.

For a moment, I'm lost. Then a small crack in the clouds lets through a glimmer of dawn light. The water beside me shimmers. I feel peace and rightness and I know that I'm almost there now. I take a few more steps along the dirt track until I come to a meadow of wallaby grass. There, beneath a flowering tea-tree shrub, is a man asleep, his head on his backpack, his old coat for a blanket.

The just-rightness dissipates, leaving only the mess of the ordinary world where I must make my own guesses.

Soft treading through the grass towards the sleeper, I half believe that it is Gardner, waiting for the sun. I crouch beside him and see Faulk's sleeping face; smoother, younger than I've known it. I see then that even devils must sleep and that for those hours they can be angels too.

I reach out to touch him, but he opens his eyes. For a moment, we see each other. Then his eyes widen and he jumps up.

"Anna!"

"Where are you going?"

"Away, outta here. Anywhere."

"You made me a promise, Faulk."

He begins rolling up his coat, stuffing it into his backpack. "How did you find me?"

"Agreements made...the way we made ours...are powerful, potent."

"Dog on a leash?"

"That kind of thing."

He slings his bag onto his back.

"All right."

The cloud is lifting with an eerie speed, bringing in another unerringly bright day. The sun hits his eyes and he blinks away from it.

"But we've got a little problem."

I raise my eyebrows and fold my arms.

"I'm not gonna be welcome at my boss's without bringing along a party gift."

"What does he need?"

"You."

"I took that as a given."

He shrugs. "You sure?"

"I am. She's my daughter."

"Let's get walking then."

"Can't we take a transport?"

"Nope. Lost my tracker ID."

He rolls up his pant leg and shows me a wad of bandage across a wound with dried blood around the edges.

"You got it out! What did you do that for?"

"You ever had one?"

"Yes. They permanently deactivated it when I left the city."

"Then you're luckier than most. They think they've got it nailed, this life. That all the good is coming their way and all they have to pay for it is their freedom. That's all. Such a little thing. They're hardly gonna miss what they've never had, but you've *had* freedom, Anna, you know it. You're not caged like these circus rats. So don't tell me you don't get why I had to do it."

There's so much I want to say that I can't speak. How little he knows about cages.

Instead, I adjust my pack and step out onto the track. "Let's just get walking."

16

FAULK

She's striding ahead of me, her green shoes crunching on gravel. Her body in motion is mesmerising. I begin to think we've always been on this road together, on this journey. That I was never desperate and alone. I want to stop and pull her down amongst the trees, to feel her against me again. But I know she'd fight like a wildcat, know it was a once and only thing she gave to me, or that I took. I'm not clear in my head which it was.

Instead, I look down at the path and think about her little girl, about how I'm going to pull it off. Whether Goldengass will find out I'm off-grid.

She stops walking and I almost crash into her. She's scanning the trees as though she's heard something. I listen hard, hoping it's not what I think it is, but I can't hear a thing. She turns to me, alert.

"What is it?"

"I thought...no, it was nothing."

I almost tell her about the dingo, but something stops me,

something I can't really put a name to. We continue on, the waterbirds filling in the silence for us.

Leaving the peace of the wetland feels like an assault. Everything is silver and flicker and colour. Despite the strict visual advertising protocols, businesses still find a way. Ideas of 'harmonious with the city's vision' seem a pure matter of taste.

We're within 100 metres of the compound when I figure some restraints are in order. I pull out the cuffs and it feels as though we've come full circle. She's compliant, allowing me to click them on.

"Now if you'd let me do this at the start..."

"We wouldn't have got to know each other so well."

I'm surprised by the humour in her voice at this late hour, figure it's some kind of off-kilter relief.

"You do know you're not getting out of this alive?"

She meets my gaze. I'm dropping her in it. She knows it. Anything for her kid.

"But Freya will," she says, "and you will make sure that happens."

It's not even a request. I don't know whether to admire her ferocious mother instinct or to balk at her tone with me.

"And then what?"

"Make sure she's safe. Take her to my father. Charles Drake; 35 Tenner Boulevarde, Beachside. He's an important man, he'll look after her."

I frown. "And when she asks about you?"

"Tell her...tell her that I love her. To be brave and to trust her gut."

Without thinking, I reach out and bring her into my arms, holding her there, feeling her warmth and aliveness. I am sending her to the grave as surely as I did the others, but I've never done it like this before.

She is the first to break free.

"There's another thing. If you see my dog, he's a dingo, please take him to my father's too. Freya loves him more than anything." Her eyes are filling with water now, as though this last request has taken all the fight out of her.

I hold her cuffed hands as we enter the compound. The silence is wrong. The doors swing open onto a courtyard with no signs of life. A scheduled rainfall event begins: light, even-sized droplets falling from a blue sky. The broad grey paving stones get slick and dark. By the time we reach the other side, cold water is trickling down the back of my neck, but I'm not sure if that's why I shiver.

We enter through the glass doors, and I lead her towards the velvet room. Up ahead, something large and dark lies lengthwise across the hall, only a few paces from the door. I know what it is as soon as the smell hits us, a smell of fear and blood and excrement. Anna wrenches herself from my grip and brings her hands up to cover her nose.

"Stay here," I tell her.

I draw my weapon and walk forward. The cell guard is flung out across the floor. There's a red mush of a hole at his jugular, his head and torso are lying in a pool of congealed blood, and there's a raw, bony stump where his right hand had once been.

"Don't come!" I call back to her. "I'm going to check the room."

I open the door to Goldengass's study. The curtains are drawn and the lamps are cold. I switch on a light and scan the room, half expecting, hoping, to find him sprawled on his face in the darkness. But there's no sign of Goldengass. Of course not.

I re-join Anna. She looks pale.

"What happened here?"

I have my ideas, but I don't share them with her.

"I don't know, but Goldengass is gone."

"And Freya?"

"Let's find out."

I uncuff her and guide her down the winding staircase into the warren. The air is dank and heavy. When we finally reach Freya's cell, we find the door wide open and the cell empty. Anna runs in and kneels down, brings one of the yellowed cushions to her chest, her body a sculpture of anguish.

I wrench my gaze from her and scan the room. I can't see the girl's stone. That she had enough time to gather up that little token gives me some small hope that she wasn't snatched. Then I find the book. It's lying open behind the bucket, with a corner of the page folded down. I pick it up, and as I read it, a kind of triumph fizzes through me.

"I thought I could, I thought I could."

"What are you saying?" She's watching me with defeated eyes.

"That she's okay!" I show her the page, but she shakes her head, not understanding. "Somebody came here to rescue her."

"Somebody other than us?" She speaks the words to herself.

"Your father?"

She shakes her head and stands up. I can see hope reigniting within her, rocketing her into action.

"We have to go! Show me the way back up."

When we reach the stairs, she races in front of me. I follow her up into the light.

She's pacing in circles by the time I find her outside the compound on the street. Her eyes are distant, as though she's concentrating on something I can't see. I stand back and watch her weaving tighter and tighter circles, sending off taut waves of frustration. Then she stops.

"It's not working. Faulk, I need to be on my own. I can't find her like this."

I say nothing. She stands before me, almost apologetic. "You've done what you can. I think we're even, don't you?"

I cross my arms. "Fair. Square. Released."

She makes as if to go and then turns back to me.

"Thank you."

"No need to thank a coward and a liar."

"But there is. Thank you."

I feel a pull in my chest as she starts walking away, something tugging at me that won't let go. So I use the only card I have left to bring her back.

"I saw your dingo."

She turns around.

"It jumped me. I thought it was going to rip out my throat."

She goes cold. "And you only thought to tell me this now?"

"I just told you I was a coward and a liar."

"Where did you see it?"

"Back at the wetlands."

She gazes back from where we've come, then nods and turns away.

I'd rather the sting of her disappointment than her distance, her preoccupation.

"What's with the dog, anyway?" I goad her to bring her back to me.

She looks at me, but it's a looking through me; she's drifting away: a helium balloon whose string I've accidentally released. I see it so clearly in that vacant space, that chasm between us: that I am nothing and no-one to her. After all I've done.

I feel a wave of violence, adrenaline flooding through me. I want to shake her, overpower her, consume her. I step up into her face.

"The thing almost killed me!"

I grab her arm. She can feel the dark energy rising in me, I'm sure of it, and tries to wrest herself from my grip. She shakes free, but as soon as she does, I grab her again, pull her against me and press my mouth roughly onto hers. She yanks her head back. I hold her tight, and the feel of the wiry muscles of her back moving beneath my hands as she tries to push me away makes me want her even more.

"You should have died. I should have died. Come on. We're alive. Can't you fucking feel it? Alive."

"Faulk, no." Her voice is barely above a whisper.

I release her. I don't know how, but I do. I want more, so much more of her, but I'm being pulled into a morass; a spiralling heap of self-hatred.

"I'm sorry," I say.

But she is shaking her head, side to side in an eternal no.

I reach out to her.

She swipes at me. "Go!"

I step back, but I don't leave.

"*Go!*"

I hunch against the dusk and walk off down the street, every part of me on fire.

17

GARDNER

$\mathcal{M}$eiying is stroking Freya's hair and singing. Through canine vision, I watch her slender fingers moving in time with her song. My daughter is lying with her head resting on Meiying's lap, her eyes closed and her body in its first ticks and twitches of sleep. I am curled on the floor beside them, the smell of blood still iron-heavy in my nostrils. Renshu is clattering in the kitchen, cleaning up from their meal. I release a heavy breath and tuck my nose under my paw. I will rest now, rest until I can become a man.

The pull of the setting sun wakes me up. The house is quiet and smells of sleep. I can hear Freya's even breathing from the spare bedroom. I get to my feet, push open the front door and trot away from the dim glow of the house, out into the wide desert where the sun is molten on the horizon. As I change, I try to release Anna's betrayal and my own brutal response to it; to shed it all with my wild form so that it might leave me a more civilised man. But standing naked beneath the sun, its meagre warmth doing nothing for me, I find I've not succeeded in forgetting the smell of her on him, or how easily I would justify his murder.

His murder, yes. I want that. And somebody knows it.

But I did not kill the guard. How sound the reasons would have been: I would have freed my daughter. And yet, I did not kill the guard. I didn't need to. Someone had been there before me. Someone who surely wants the world to know me as the beast I am.

I am thankful. So deeply thankful to have my Freya back with me. But I'm afraid of what deeper designs are at work. Afraid of who might want to put me in the frame.

And there is something else that sits amongst my thoughts like a bloated leech. Something I don't want to see but whose insistent itch I must pay heed to, something that says I would have done it, for Freya; and worse still, that I might have enjoyed it—the blood and the disaster, the shaking and ripping of a man so that his life ebbs away in my mouth. That the wildness in me has been roused and is not yet satiated.

I walk under the night, my bare feet sinking into the warm sand, my body soaking up starlight, such starlight. The sky is more silver than black here; the milky way a broad shining cloth in the moon-dark night. I howl, releasing the dingo from me so that it can run across the globe and return to me in the morning. The constellations watch me and Orion aims his bow below the horizon, pointing lazily at a dingo's spirit.

Anna. My thoughts return to her. The beast that I was knew so much as I breathed in her essence on the stranger. I could smell her fear on him, the unfamiliar fragrance of her shampoo—layered, costly and rich, and a scent suggesting she'd been complicit, or at least not unwilling. I could also smell, beneath it all, the bargain she'd struck with her body.

Understood what she'd given for Freya. I knew so much then.

Yet, as the man I am now, I can't help but feel wounded, can't help but feel the simple and powerful pain of betrayal.

I run. Saltbush spikes my feet. Cold air sinks from the sky and seeps up from the ground. I run and run, trying to wash it all out, to bring my heart to gratitude before I enter Meiying and Renshu's home again.

When I return, they are waiting at the door. Meiying holds out some clothes for me, her face solemn. I thank her in surprise and put them on. They fit well enough. Renshu's eyes are wide as he watches me.

"Meiying told me, but I did not believe."

"Few can see so clearly," I say, and Meiying smiles.

"My wife is a rare being indeed!" Renshu throws an arm around her shoulder and ushers me inside.

In the warm living-room I settle into an armchair with a glass of some sort of spirit proffered by Renshu.

I can hear the sounds of his cooking in the kitchen now: pots clanking onto the stove-top, the sluicing of tap-water, and his rapid-fire cutting of some vegetable on a wooden board.

Meiying studies me in silence, and it is a distinctly knowing gaze. Eventually she leans forward and speaks, her voice low and solemn beneath the kitchen clatter:

"You wish to kill a man."

I feel the heat drain from my face and my heart start up a heavy thunder.

She shakes her head and places her hand on mine.

"Do not allow the bloodwork to take hold within you. Your daughter deserves a man she can have pride in."

Renshu walks in with a tray. We watch in silence as he fills small cups with steaming jasmine tea. Meiying picks one up, holds it in both her hands and passes it to me. I bow my head.

"Thank you."

She nods. "You are welcome."

IN THE MORNING, I wake well before dawn. My night was a strange and restless one as I tried to sleep on a mattress beside Freya. Even on the floor, it felt too soft for the traveller and the beast within me.

I find my way to the kitchen where Meiying stands stirring something steaming on the stove.

"Congee?" She scoops some into a bowl.

I nod my thanks and take it from her. The taste is sweet and light and I can feel its heat trickling into all the places that need warming inside me.

"Let me show you something," she says, "come on, you can bring that."

I follow her through a room at the back of the house and out into a glassed-off area; a kind of conservatory wrapped around three faces of the house. She switches on some down lights and I see that the place is filled with a verdant array of plants. We wander through and I recognise some of them—ginger lilies, orchids—but there are many more I've never seen; tropical, broad-leaved trees reaching to the roof, laden with strange fruits. A huge, irregularly shaped pond takes up most of the east side. Water trickles down its slick rocks, and flowering water-lilies layer its surface. A many-fingered ring of black-leaved taro plants lines the inner edge, and its outer edge is fringed by berries on drooping canes. Meiying picks a handful of raspberries for me. They are sweet and tangy in my mouth.

"How do you do this in the desert? Without power, without anything?"

"We *have* power. From the sun. We don't need any complicated photosyn technology. It just comes through our window, and we collect it. The plants do the rest for us. We have solar panels and storage for the night though." She smiles. "We're low-tech, not no tech."

"And you grow all your food here?"

"Most of it. We get some long-lasting staples we can't grow ourselves from the market, and it's a bit of fun to go there, adds some variety."

"Impressive."

"People are so afraid, Gardner. They can't see what can be done. Our sickness was our learning, our initiation into a life that had to be led differently. I'm old enough to remember when we still had a choice; a choice to retreat into ourselves, or to grow and learn.

"Renshu and I chose to be out here, to be part of the study, to get away from what the Dome people call life. But let me tell you something Gardner: we are in the control group. We weren't given the Life Extension Therapy; they gave us the placebo. We're not supposed to know that, but we do. It took some digging, but we found out. And look at us. It is *living* that is working for us. Living. Joy. Love. Don't forget these things."

I feel the first long ray of the waking sun.

"You have a choice too, Gardner."

Light floods the conservatory with a brilliance that blinds me.

I lift off my clothes. My body melts and shifts. And it occurs to me as I turn from man to dingo that perhaps the beast was never my canine form. More beastly things have been done by human nature.

Meiying is standing before me, watching, smiling. Behind her, I hear green things whispering and I can smell their potency. I search for something more than human about her, but I do not find it. She is deeply earthly, a thing of humanity, both human and humane. I bow my head. She strokes my coat. A human who has chosen kindness. Nothing more and nothing less than that.

Freya eats as though she's never eaten before. Meiying laughs as she serves her a second bowl. Renshu is chopping long green stalks that I don't recognise to make into a soup with ginger and chilli and garlic. When she has finished her food, Freya joins me on the floor and curls against my side.

"Daddy, I missed you so much."

Her body feels bony against mine. I lick her cheek. I can't help thinking of her filthy cell. I know it does no good, but I keep returning to it like a festering wound. I wish for words, to be a man like any other, so that I can hold her in my arms and tell her she is safe now, safe with me. I put a paw over her and she closes her eyes.

18

ANNA

*I*t is a hard morning. Its light too bright, its edges cold and grey. I don't think I slept. If I did, it was only a restless twitching in the crevice I'd wedged myself into, hermit-crab-like, overnight. I walk now, a human animal, searching only for sustenance. Blue with cold and hunger, I follow a footpath leading into the city like a vein into a heart. I am Anna Drake. I am Anna Drake. I pass under a billboard beaming my father's product into the universe. *'Photosyntech Corporation...Biology for life.'* Charles Drake, developer of the Dome's life-sustaining technologies. *'We'll keep you safe'.*

A chilly wind blows across an empty square, unusually cold for the Dome. Someone having a frolic at weather control, perhaps, losing concentration for a moment. It is icy, but it wakes me up.

I walk to a free coffee station and tap the requisite buttons. It is good and hot. Aromatic, no bitterness, just the right amount of micro foam. I remember the baristas and their latte art protests. I look at my perfect cup that no human hand has touched save mine and at the deserted plaza, built for people and laughter, and I wonder why *that* all had to go? It was no prerequisite that people shouldn't mingle in the street in our new city. But the street is no longer a patch on the world within. Love is made with 'Sex Inc.', happiness with 'Joy'. The world inside our minds is the place where life occurs.

I sit on a recycled plastic seat curved into the shape of a sprouting seed frozen in its unfurling. They had such dreams, such hope, the people who made this. My father had been one of them, had embraced the optimism of the first Dome generation. This was to be a paradise, a new start, a place where people could live in ecological balance and survive in a world trashed by their forefathers.

Charles Drake was one of the early tinkerers. He had emerged from the wellspring of new thinkers searching for a viable alternative technology, one that could supersede the old fossil fuel industries and support a new way of living. He'd been a man driven by a vision.

He and my mother had both been part of that generation of ecological dreamers. They had shared so much at first, but then the Dome Construction Authority adopted his technology. As his wealth accrued, so did his status. By increments, his standards and ideas shifted, and soon, perhaps without fully realising it, he became a part of the establishment. My mother's continued questioning of the status quo now seemed to threaten all he had worked to build.

I was very young, but I still remember the fights, the sharp edges to my father's words, even though I didn't understand their content. My relief when he went away was not natural for a child so young; I see that now. But I never missed him. And my mother was so much happier, so much more peaceful without him. Her warmth, her deep, calm love, was more than enough to carry me through.

I could go back to my father now. *No.* The thought is a bubble of insanity. I made my choice when I left against his will, and I doubt he'd be so kindly disposed to me a second time. Besides, the thought of his home like a gilded cell is enough to send me fleeing back to the desert.

I could spiral around the city forever trying to find some trace of Freya. Or I could trust that against all odds she is safe, that somehow Gardner found a way to free them both. And I could carry on.

I get up, caffeine coaxing my body into action, lending me its alien energy. Now I have the address from the Library database. That had been the one missing piece, the piece Gardner had carried for us. How easily we'd laid our plans that night the breeze lifted our maps and Freya's soft snoring echoed from my mother's cave-walled bedroom. How loftily I'd ignored the possibility that we might become separated. How unprepared I really was.

I stare at the street map shimmering in the air in front of me. It disappears. I tap the wall again. Study it until I think I know the way. A girl, the first child I've seen for days, is waiting patiently behind me. She watches me with bright, curious eyes as I step aside for her. I scan the thin stream of passers-by. No one seems to be waiting for her.

"Are you okay?"

She nods.

"Where are your parents?"

She taps the wall and then points to a private car idling silently by the curb. Through the window I can see a woman, her face pale and vacant, staring at the floating pods above us. I turn back to the girl who sighs; a strangely adult sound.

"It's all right, Mummy's just had too much Calm again. I'm taking her to Daddy."

"On your own?"

"Yes, it's all right. Daddy lets me. Wish they'd let me have Mapping though, then I wouldn't have to do this. He's at a meeting." Her finger hovers over the map. "Oh good, it's not far." She glances at me. "I have to go."

Then she runs back to the car and jumps in. It melds slickly into the traffic.

I have forgotten which way I need to go and when I bring up the map again, my hand is shaking. Her composure was like Freya's, like a child grown too quickly; some aspects of her stretched to adult proportions, some still coiled with the potential of a baby.

I try to keep the directions in mind as I walk, but Freya's serious face is haunting me. What kind of mother have I been? She'd never been one to run with the other kids, to just be silly. I'd always thought the wildness of desert life was enough; the way she'd sprint across the sand as though it didn't suck at her heels, the way she'd track lizards to their homes, scale rocks at The Gorge and jump into the ground-water chill of Green Lake…I thought all that was enough. I thought the warm heart and embrace of her parents was enough. But she was never quite a child. Even as a baby, she'd studied my face as though it held all the secrets in the world and she was intent on unravelling them. *Oh Freya. We should have stayed. Let you be.*

I reach the turnoff into the old stone laneway sooner than I'd expected. A dull thud of a base drum issues from the first house on the street and I realise I haven't heard that sound at street level for so long. I look along the laneway. There are no pods here, only old-style townhouses from the city's pre-Dome days. Vertical gardens cover the walls in green.

Photosyn veins run up between them to second-storey apartments. Without these additions, this street would have probably looked very much the same a hundred years ago.

The house is about half-way along. The iron gate opens easily and soon I'm leaping up the cracked concrete steps to stand in front of a white door with a round, black knocker.

I hammer twice, my heart thumping. After a minute, just as I'm wondering whether to knock again, I hear a latch being turned from inside. I feel her presence before I can truly see who is standing there. It's like a wild blast of a sea-wind in my face, forcing me to close my eyes. When I open them, I think at first that it's Shama and my heart leaps with a fierce joy. But then I see that the woman peering at me is older than Shama, and despite my first impression, is nothing like her.

She is tiny. Dark hair, streaked with white, frames a round face with a pointed chin. Black eyes glint above a thin nose and taut, flat cheeks. Her mouth is a small, perfect thing. I find myself mesmerised by her quartz-white teeth as she speaks to me.

"Within the mother the seed, within the child the mother."

"Dr Kuanyin? I'm Anna."

"Hello Anna. Come in. Please, call me Lin."

I follow Lin through an almost dark hallway to the end of her house. She ushers me into a large room flooded with green-tinged sunlight. A trellis outside her window, thick with an old grapevine in young leaf, lends the room the quality of a clearing in a forest.

"Please, take a seat." She points to an ancient armchair and shuffles off through a nearby door.

I sit and watch the dust I've unsettled spiral up into a swirling vortex. From the kitchen, I can hear water being poured, teaspoons clinking against glass, but everything else is silence. There is serenity here; a sense of long, golden hours slowly and surely ticking by.

She returns with two glasses filled with steaming liquid, black on the bottom, white on the top.

"Liquorice tea," she says, "quells the hunger while we talk." I take it, dubious, but hungry enough to try it.

She sits in an armchair opposite me, crosses her legs and chugs down her tea as though it's the last beer before closing. Then she dabs her mouth with a small, perfectly folded white handkerchief.

"So, where is the child?"

I try to explain, but end up shaking my head, the upwelling of all of it threatening to spill over into tears. She leans forward and pats my leg.

"No matter. No matter. Drink up."

I take a sip and the strange ice-heat spice of liquorice spreads across my tongue and tingles pleasantly down my throat. She watches me.

There is a sudden, loud bang. I jump. Tea slops over my hand. Something has crashed into the window. I spin around to the source of the sound. At first, I think a bird has flown into the glass. But then I see that a bat-like creature has attached itself to the window with something that looks horribly like a fleshy sucker. The old woman puts a finger to her lips and shakes her head, rising to slide open the door onto the back patio while I force down a scream.

"Zotzi, what are you doing?" She sounds annoyed but not afraid.

The creature detaches itself from the glass and flies into her arms. She cradles it to her as though it's a baby, and it buries its head under her arm.

"Come on, then." She carries it inside and sits down again.

I look at the quivering, black-furred creature in her arms, at its leathery wings that are stretching and folding, for all the world like a cat getting comfortable on its owner's lap.

"What is that?" I try not to sound as panicky as I feel, but the scream's still in my throat, trying to come out.

"They called him 'Nightspawn'—a cruel, unjust name. Zotzi lives with me now." She lowers her voice and leans in. "Parents couldn't quite cope. You'll have to excuse him. He hates missing out. You know what five-year-olds are like." The creature huffs in her arms and she strokes its head. "Yes, you're a big kid, but you've still got a lot to learn." She looks up at me inquiringly. "So—your daughter."

I can't quite tear my gaze from Zotzi as I try to refocus on the questions Gardner and I had wanted answers to so many weeks ago.

"My daughter, Freya, is...a different child." I'm suddenly nervous, my mouth dry. I take a sip of the tea, but its metallic sweetness on the back of my tongue makes me nauseous.

"Go on," says Lin.

"I...her father and I believe she will soon undergo a transformation. Of a kind that we've been led to believe is your area of specialty."

Lin nods. "It is." She looks down at Zotzi, whose eyes have closed beneath her stroking fingers. "First, her ancestry."

"Ancestry?"

Lin meets my eyes, her gaze shrewd and unblinking. "Tell me about your side of the family."

"It's not me. It's Gardner, her father." My voice is barely above a whisper.

Lin peers at me, bird-like. "It's nothing to be ashamed of."

I nod. "It's just, we decided...he decided really, that it would be best, easier, if his Changes were kept a secret."

Lin raises her eyebrows.

"Her father is, well...at night he's a man, and during the day, a dingo."

Lin nods again and strokes Zotzi. "Yes, yes, and sunset and sunrise trigger his Change." Zotzi snores softly in her lap. "It's not unheard of. Zotzi is also a Spiritwalker like your Gardner"

"Spiritwalker?"

"Yes. His parents were not at all prepared. Neither of them could imagine or accept such a life. They refused to acknowledge that it was an inherited trait, even believed he wasn't their own son. In Zotzi's case, the gift skipped a generation. Zotzi's grandfather was a deeply conservative man who'd apparently attempted to have his wife, a Spiritwalker, committed on several occasions. Eventually, this woman left her husband, evidently without revealing her secret to her daughter. The daughter, Zotzi's mother, grew up sharing her father's moral persuasions—persuasions that, sadly, could not encompass having a Spiritwalker for a son."

"How many Spiritwalkers are there out there?"

"It's hard to tell, as they often keep their ability to Change a secret. I don't believe there are many. There are still some who can transform at will and are not confined to their spirit form during the daylight hours. These are becoming rarer though. Zotzi and Gardner are not this wild type."

"Oh! Why can't they shift when they want to? It would...it would change everything if Gardner could."

Lin shakes her head sadly. "Something happened several generations ago. A mutation, or an attempt to control the Spiritwalkers, perhaps. I don't know for sure. But your Gardner and Zotzi here are descended from those with more confined abilities."

A growing sadness washes through me as she talks and I watch the sleeping creature in her arms.

"Gifts are often passed down matrilineally," she continues.

It takes the silence that follows for me to register Lin's words. I look from Zotzi to her dark, scrutinising eyes.

"Through the mother?"

Lin nods slowly. "You are waiting for Freya to take on her father's shape-shifting trait, to become a Spiritwalker; but what of the blood of the mother? Years of memory are stored within the thread that weaves red and wild from woman to woman. You yourself are a storehouse for such gifts."

I bring my fingers to my temples, rub at the ache building there, and try to think through the fog of exhaustion and confusion. Lin's sharp gaze does not let up and I begin to feel that she's burrowing into my mind. She well could be, for all I know.

"Well, I don't have any gifts," I say finally. "There's nothing different about me."

"You are sure of this?"

Her challenge goads something awake within me. "Yes, I am. It's not me!" Zotzi startles awake. I'm shouting. How can I be shouting?

She raises her neat, black eyebrows.

"All right," she strokes Zotzi back to sleep, "let's focus on your daughter."

I nod, not trusting myself to speak. The raw loss hits me again and I cradle my stomach as it contracts with the pain of it.

"I lost her." I whisper.

Lin's voice is soft and hard, twined like a snake and a vine. "Yes. And you will find her."

I press my forehead to my knees, trying to stop the tears from welling up.

I feel Lin's hand at my back. "Here." She's holding a small vial of clear liquid. "To help you focus. Just a sip will do."

I sit up and bring some of the liquid into my mouth. It's cold and tasteless. I swallow.

"Zotzi and I will leave you now to do your work. Call for me when you're done."

She turns away, but I shake my head and reach for her. *Don't go!* But I can't speak because there's a sudden pain in my core that feels like a breath-sucking punch. I fall into the armchair, my body rigid.

I am turning, turning—a child on a grassy field; feet lifting and shifting, lifting and shifting. I try to see through the blur, but I can't, and the lurching and twisting is making me queasy. So I stop. But the ground doesn't, and I fall.

I open my eyes to a world of bright mist. I squint into it, trying to make something out of the branching forms swirling around me. Gradually, the mist clears and the spinning stops and I'm standing on a hilltop with pale grass beneath my feet and the sky around me like a sea. Three twisted eucalypts squatting against the blaze of a midday sun are the only break in the vast view of a wide, blue sky, and the air shimmers with a heat I can't feel.

I hear deep wingbeats, the shift of feather on feather; a keratin slicing of the air. A wedge-tailed eagle lifts from below and begins circling above me. Hot and cold memories of Faulk's touch shiver through me. With each circle, I get another flash. I am there again on his kitchen floor, with his life and heat spilling inside me. I cry out, try to swipe the eagle away, try to stop the simultaneous flood of fear and exhilaration. My blood is roaring in my ears, deafening me. His hands on me had been fierce. What in me had wanted it?

What had I wanted? Power over him? The subjugation of my own power?

Or had I just wanted my daughter back?

"Stop!" I shout to the eagle. It dips as though doffing a cap at me and lands on the grass. It is a huge, bright, talonous creature.

"Are we dead?" I ask the eagle.

The bird shifts and shimmers, shrugs off its feather cloak until it is a woman, sitting with her knees bent up and her head facing down. She looks up from beneath a black waterfall of hair and as she straightens, I see that in her naked arms, asleep against her breast, is a tiny newborn baby with hair as dark as her own.

"We are," she says. "But you are not. Not yet."

I stare at her.

"He is lost," she says.

"Who is?"

"Faulk."

My skin prickles.

"We loved him." Her voice is a sigh.

I bring my hands to my mouth and shake my head.

"Are you...Mia?" I whisper the absurd question through my fingers.

She nods, bringing her baby's doll-like hand into her own. "And this is Orion."

Afraid that she might turn back into mist and feather, I speak softly: "He said you never got a chance to name him."

"He didn't. But I did."

She fixes me with her dark brown eyes and I feel as though she's tunnelling through me somehow, feeling all that I felt: his lips across my skin, his weight, the hard floor beneath me. I shiver. She watches me, and I suddenly fear what power the vengeful dead could have in this place.

"I'm sorry." My words sound hollow, insipid. I reach for something more. "He still loves you. He's hurting and grieving for you. I don't know him well, but even I can see that."

"You have known him well enough." Her voice is brittle and laced with bitterness.

My heart kicks up a beat and I feel blood rise to my face. "You are a mother—what would you not do for your child?"

"I never got to be a mother. I do not know."

My stomach clenches. I try to catch her gaze, to will her to see how it was with us the last time her beloved and I met, how close to the edge he had been and how I still do not know if the wrongness was within him or within me. Shame and anger build like spiralling pillars within me. I want her to know, to understand, to forgive. To help me forgive.

But Mia looks down at her child and does not oblige me.

"He is not the man you knew," I say. And I am not the woman I knew.

She laughs, and there's no humour in it. "No. He is not."

Neither of us speaks, and the blue, heatless sky is all there is.

"Why am I here? What do you want from me?" I'm not sure if I've spoken the words or merely thought them into the silence.

She hears them though; she lifts her head and raises her eyebrows coolly.

"I, from you? You summoned me." Her expression is aloof, her air regal. When I can't find words, she frowns and speaks slowly and clearly: "What is it *you* want from *me*?"

The answer swells and bursts into the air between us. "I want to find my family—my daughter, Freya and her father, Gardner."

Mia fixes me once more with her gaze. I can't tell what emotion is circling within her. Finally, she speaks again.

"They're not here. They remain in the world of the living."

"Can you...see...anything more? See where they are?"

She shakes her head. "You've journeyed too deeply. Your fear brought you here. You need to re-enter your world and use your gift there." Her face softens. "Good luck."

"Thank you." I feel an urge to reach out and touch her, but my heart, insistently alive in this world of the dead, warns me against it. "And...I am so sorry."

She nods, ever so slightly, and then recedes from me into the mist. The world spins again; the hill and the eucalypts vanish and I fall heavily against the back of the armchair.

I open my eyes and wait for the room to right itself.

"Lin!"

19

GARDNER

*I*t was never a choice, really. I toy with the idea of leaving her, of going home, paw at it like it's a mouse, all tumble and tail in the dust. In the end, though, I don't have the heart. I will go back to the Dome and look for Anna.

In my dreams, Anna is slipping between the trees as I try to follow her. I only want to talk to her. But he is there, blocking my way. I can smell the fight in his sweat and her scent all over him. All the hairs on my coat are on end and I bare my teeth. It's his warm blood in my mouth that wakes me up.

"Daddy!" Freya is bouncing on me. She catches my tail beneath her knees and I yelp and twist onto all fours. "Come on!" she shouts. "It's breakfast time."

Freya runs out of the bedroom and I lope along behind her into the bright living room. She clambers onto a chair at the table where Renshu and Meiying are laying down placemats and bowls, platters of fruit and a plate of steaming noodles. I snuffle towards the smell. Meiying places a dish on the ground for me and fills it with food from the table. As I gobble it up, soaking in the soothing flow of Meiying and Renshu's voices and Freya's chatter, I try to map out my journey in my mind.

I'm tempted to take up our hosts' offer of leaving Freya with them and returning in their car to the Dome. Renshu has been keeping an ear out for any alerts with their emergency headset. At present, all is quiet, so he figures they're unlikely to be checking passengers. I find it unnerving that more hasn't been made of our escape; but then, someone made it easy for us. I have no doubt the entries and exits are being closely guarded, though. The only card we have up our sleeve is that there is nothing at all to connect us with Meiying and Renshu.

I sit on my haunches and watch them eating and laughing with Freya. Do I really want to put these kind people at risk? It astonishes me they'd even offer, gamble all they have made here, their very lives, for veritable strangers. I don't understand it, and yet it warms me to the core. If I don't take up their offer, there is little chance of returning to Anna unscathed.

And there is abandoning Freya again. To be apart from her so soon after her ordeal. It's a bitter choice to make. Since we arrived here in that race across the city and back out to the Market, after the frantic search of the campground hoping to track down Meiying and Renshu, and the sheer fluke of finding their trail, I had sworn to myself to that I would provide Freya with only peace and safety from now on. Yet, after my restless night of hauntings and huntings, I know this is something I cannot do, not yet. *Damn you, Anna!* For a moment, I despise her for driving me to leave our child. But it is his scent that has left the most bitter taste in my mouth.

Freya is no longer laughing. It's the silence that makes me look towards the table. She's holding Meiying's hand, watching Renshu, who has his hand to his ear and is listening with rapt stillness.

"Reports of Silk Moths coming this way."

My ears prick, and I sniff at the air.

"When are they coming, Renshu?" Meiying asks him, her voice slipping under the current of fear in the room, barely disturbing the air.

His gaze locks on hers. "Now."

Freya stares up at Meiying. "What do we do?"

"You and your daddy have to leave," she says gently.

I rise to all fours, exchanging a glance with Meiying. She nods and begins gathering up the remains of the meal.

"Gardner!" I realise I'm pacing. I stop. "Take this food. Take our car. Take Freya with you. If trouble comes our way, we can always walk to our neighbour's house, borrow their horse if need be."

Freya starts to cry.

"We'll be all right," says Meiying, clasping Freya's hand. "And so will you be."

Within minutes, we're outside by the car. Meiying and Renshu squat so that they're at Freya's height and they both hug her. She closes her eyes, squeezes her cheek against Meiying's shoulder and rests for a moment in the warm circle of their arms. Then Renshu lifts her up and places her gently into the seat. I jump up next to her and Meiying slides our packs in after me.

"I've set it to driverless. Touch here for return mode when you don't need it anymore," says Renshu, and then ducks out of the car. I fix them both with a gaze that I hope conveys everything I feel, sending my gratitude to them as best I can. Renshu nods and closes the door. They wave as the car moves off.

Half an hour into the drive, the first Moth appears on the horizon. Our car whizzes towards them. Freya rests against me, her face glazed with tiredness. When she spots them, she sits up, her eyes opening wide. It's an entire platoon of Silk Moths. We've seen the cars before: black, with the Dome Protection logo, a silk moth in a red circle, painted on their front and sides.

I hope against hope that they'll ignore us purely because of the direction we're travelling; surely the last thing they'd expect is for us to to be heading back into the Dome. But I nudge Freya down anyway and press us both flat against the seat. She buries her face into my fur and lies still, her heart thundering.

I hold my breath as the flash and shadow of each car in the platoon passes. The occupants can't look in on us because their vehicles are low slung, built for road-hugging speed, but as our lone car slides alongside them, this is small reassurance; at any moment, I expect to hear a car pulling out of the platoon and screeching a U-turn up behind us. Even after the last car has passed, we remain frozen against the seat for a long time.

"Daddy?"

Freya's whisper rouses me, finally, to raise my nose to the window and peer outside. Dead sugar gums line the highway like white ghost dancers and granite boulders rest across the land like a giant's abandoned petanque set. There is no sign of the Silk Moths.

I lift my paw off her and poke my muzzle under her armpit to help her back up onto the seat. She twines her fingers into my fur and grips on. I lean against her and we both look out the window at the parched land speeding by.

It's not long before the Dome comes into view. It sits like a jellyfish on the horizon, looming larger by the second as we hurtle towards it. I can almost feel its contained hostility, its defiance of the landscape. It is a pulsating, deadly thing; a pustule on the barren skin of earth.

Freya is snoring lightly against me. I look down at her sleep-slumped body, all brown limbs and tangled hair, her palms open, her little fingers eased from their clutching of my fur, her nails brown with desert dirt. She has lengthened since we started out, and shows no vestige of the toddler she was such a short time ago. Now, most definitely a kid.

My heart kicks as I get a sudden flash of memory from a long-ago hike up at The Gorge. Anna had gone ahead of us, huffed from a fight. I don't even remember what it was about, but during those early baby days of sleep deprivation and constant vigilance, there'd been many. Eventually, Freya and I had reached a sandstone bluff overlooking a chasm of tumble-down boulders and a roaring black river. Anna was nowhere to be seen. I'd sniffed at the air to check on her direction, swivelled into the wind to gather her scent. And suddenly, there was Freya at the corner of my vision, toddling towards the edge. I leapt towards her, grabbed her with my muzzle and pulled her away just before she stepped out into the air.

For weeks, at night, I replayed that scene in my head. What if I'd been a second too late? What if? I'd break into a sweat and punch at the pillow. A second was not good enough.

Now, I look at her sleeping face and the same heat prickles my skin. This time I'm taking her to the edge myself. *Hold on to her, you mongrel, don't you dare let go.* My growl makes her twitch in her dreams.

We sail past the sleeping Night Market and reach the

Dome gate with no further incident. I'm feeling almost confident as we enter under the shining steel columns, curved inwards like the rib bones of a giant carcass, funnelling us toward the entrance. We have just entered the tunnel when the glow of our panel dims and the vehicle stops. With a jerk that wakes Freya, our car is pulled sideways towards a yawning opening in the tunnel wall. Freya clutches me, and I can feel her heartbeat quickening.

"What's happening?" She tries to whisper, but fear constricts her words into a strangled yelp. "Daddy?"

I sniff at the air. It's completely black outside the vehicle, and we're still moving sideways into the wall. Then the car comes to an abrupt halt, throwing us across the back seat. Floodlights flash on all around us, blinding us to whatever's outside the car. With a hydraulic sigh, the doors release and open of their own accord. Freya shrinks against me. A light shines into my face. Someone is shouting and waving a torch.

"Out. Get out!"

Freya screams as she's wrenched from me. I growl and howl and leap out of the car after her. Although I'm blinded by spotlights and the flashing torch, I can smell at least four men around us. Saliva rises in my mouth and I leap at the one holding Freya. My claws rake his arm and my teeth dig into his flesh. Another one runs forward out of the dark to grab Freya again as she tries to run. I leap towards them, but as I jump, I feel a sting in my side. The world blurs, my limbs become heavy and I fall to the floor.

20

GARDNER

*W*hen I open my eyes, it's to a round roof above and a soft bed beneath me. Freya lies stretched out beside me, her eyes closed, her breathing even. Along the contoured wall opposite sits a small, curved cabinet filled with coloured glass bottles. A sculpture sits on top of it—a latticework of photosyn veins, crossing and twisting into the shape of an open hand. Held in its palm is a dome, opaque with swirling mist.

I sit up, careful not to disturb Freya, and swing my legs over the edge of the bed. My bare feet sink into soft carpet. I barely allow myself to breathe as I listen for any sounds from outside the room. All is dead silence. At the end of the bed are some clothes—a dark blue shirt, brown pants, long, black boots; all strangely old-fashioned, with no outward hint of embedded tech, but new and clean, and clearly meant for me.

As I pull them on, I scan the room. There is little else to see, save two glasses and what looks like a jug of water on the bedside table. Once I'm dressed, I pour a glass and sniff at the liquid, wishing momentarily for my daytime form. With my feeble human nose, I can detect nothing out of the ordinary. I take another small sip. Nothing unusual. I drink some more, and then drain the glass in my thirst.

Our backpacks lie by the window. I go to mine and take out the container of food packed by Meiying and Renshu. It still looks and smells good to eat, which suggests we haven't been comatose too long. I shovel some noodles into my mouth and my stomach growls approvingly in response.

Pulling out the apple next, I walk across the room, crunching into it, sucking out the sweet juice as I squat in front of the sculpture. I'm mesmerised by the never-settling mist in the dome. Now that I'm close, I can see a bronze plaque at its base and I lean in to read the inscription:

'*Awarded by the Department of the Environment and Sustainable Future to Charles Drake, Founder of Photosyntech Corporation, for his great and enduring service to humanity.*'

I go to the window and rip open curtains that feel like a liquid skin beneath my fingers. Outside, it is night and the lights of the city glow below us from Charles Drake's pod.

My father-in-law never did warm to me. The first time Anna introduced us, at our commitment ceremony, I took his stern silence as merely a father's reluctance to see his daughter wed, a kind of paternal possessiveness. The second and last time we spoke, his way with me was no different, and I became less sure that his was not a more personal dislike. Admittedly, I'd contacted him in the middle of the night, without his daughter's knowledge, to ask the kind of favour no man in his position would be keen to bestow.

Soft footsteps outside have me whipping around to face the door. I glance at Freya. She hasn't stirred, and it only now occurs to me that they must have drugged her. Heat prickles up my neck and I ball up my fists as I move to stand between her and the door.

The knock is quiet and precise. The door opens and I suck in a quick breath. The last time I saw him was in the eerie, flickering light of the interface as I stood amongst the plants and sandstone tiles of our interior courtyard back home. The air had been so humid next to the trickling fountain that I'd started sweating as I whispered to the ghost glow while a pregnant Anna slept.

Charles Drake looks different tonight. Age seems to have leapt upon him with unsparing ferocity. And yet, as he walks into the room and I can see him more clearly, I realise he has no wrinkles to match the whiteness of his hair or the paleness of his skin.

His gaze is calm, scrutinising. I meet it unflinchingly.

"The clothes look well on you Gardner."

I fix him with a hard stare until his eyes flicker from mine to the prostrate form of my daughter. An uncheckable well of anger rises within me and loosens my tongue.

"What did you do to her?"

He smiles, but there is nothing warm about the glint in his eyes or the smug curve of his lips.

"It'll wear off by the morning. Until then, you and I have some things to discuss."

He turns his back on me, leaving the door open for me to follow.

Floor-to-ceiling windows create a curved corner of night in the room he's led me into. A table set with a softly glowing photosyn candle at its centre seems almost to float in the blackness.

Charles Drake pulls a chair a little way out for me.

"You needn't have eaten," he says as he seats himself opposite. "Hobbs has quite outdone himself on your account tonight."

It's disconcerting seeing the city lights at my feet as I sit down. Pods float like shark egg-cases below us and the night is dark and moonless.

"What do you want, Charles?"

"Orion is rising," says Charles, following my gaze out to the dim stars beyond the glass. "The poor hunter. Always upside down, can't quite get his bow on target. But we don't need him now, do we? We don't need his sword. We have a web. The perfection of the Dome to keep us safe and mild. We are tame creatures now. Trapped by our own delusions. I have that to be proud of."

I can feel his pale face intent on me and I suppress a shiver. Surely he's trying to set me on edge, off kilter. Or maybe this is madness; pure ravings and rantings. I look directly into his face and see neither of these things. In his eyes like deep pits, I see it—envy. Envy for my wildness, envy for the freedom I have and he doesn't. And then, in a flicker, it's gone.

He shrugs. "And who can begrudge me a little heart-to-heart with my son-in-law? Ah, thank you Hobbs."

A neat, small-faced man appears by the table and places plates with silver bell lids onto each of our settings. Hobbs lifts the lid off Charles' plate first to reveal a steaming meal of meat and vegetables. I feel my stomach rumble. He trots around to me and lifts mine off with a flourish.

A dead rabbit with bedraggled fur and glazed eyes lies limply across my plate.

I stare down at it, my jaw tightening. When I look up, it's to Charles' cold-eyed smile.

"Not to your taste tonight?"

My nostrils flare.

"I see. Perhaps you prefer this kind of meal for lunch instead." He claps his hands and the gnomish man reappears.

"Hobbs, our guest finds this a little too rare for his liking. Would you bring him something more suitable?"

"Of course, sir."

With my teeth clenched, I watch Hobbs scuttle off. Then I'm on my feet, pushing at the table, sending the chair behind me flying against the window. Unfortunately, nothing breaks.

"It was you! You had that guard killed. To make me look like an animal!"

Charles' smile is toadlike.

"What do you want from me and my daughter?" I hammer the tablecloth with my fist and feel the satisfying resistance of the wood beneath it.

Charles only raises his eyebrows. "Do you really find it so hard to contain your beastliness?"

I know he's goading me, but all the rage that has been building since Anna's betrayal sweeps through me like a red tide. I lean across the table and grab him by the throat.

"No." I grip his warm neck. "Do you?"

His composure as I tighten my grasp is unnerving, but the feel of his Adam's apple beneath my palm brings a flash of desire; for blood, hot and pulsing, spilling into my mouth. I release him.

Charles adjusts his collar and sits back. I stand there breathing heavily, staring at him as he pours himself a glass of water.

"What do you want, Charles?"

"Want? I want my daughter not to have married a base aberration of nature. But I didn't get that, did I?"

I cross my arms.

He cuts into his meat and for a moment, the only sound is the scraping of his cutlery against the plate.

Hobbs re-enters the room with another plate and swaps

it for the dead rabbit. He glances at me by the window and then at Charles.

"Everything all right, sir?"

"Quite fine, thank you Hobbs."

Hobbs lifts the lid on a perfectly decent-looking meal. My stomach growls. I wait until he has left the room before I sit down.

"That's better," says Charles. "Perhaps now we can continue our conversation in a more civilised manner."

"Just let us leave. She's your own granddaughter, for Christ's sake!"

He rests his knife and fork neatly on his plate and looks me up and down. "What does she see in you, I wonder? Anna. How does she do it?"

The food cools on my plate, and I just try to keep breathing.

"I mean, living like a raggle taggle gypsy with her mother, that's one thing, but having a child to a beast..." He sighs. "Anyway, you mustn't think me a bigot; I'm not. I'm actually rather interested in you, Gardner. I have something of a family history of interest in your kind." He picks up his cutlery again and gestures with his knife. "Go on, eat."

"I'm not hungry."

He shrugs. "Suit yourself."

"Why did you bring us here?"

"Gardner, you are my guest. Freya will be well in the morning. Please, try and relax."

I stare down at the food; saliva squirts into my mouth. I unclench my jaw, lift my fork and spear a quarter of potato. It tastes good.

Charles Drake nods and for several minutes, we eat in silence. Eventually, Charles lifts his napkin and dabs at the corners of his mouth.

"So, tell me: have you always been…like this? Did my daughter know you were only half a man before she married you?"

I'm inclined to say nothing and keep eating, but something behind his insult-riddled questioning intrigues me. It's an intangible; a whiff of a more desperate motive beneath his off-hand manner. I breathe, allow my pulse to even out, and slowly finish my mouthful. Then I place my cutlery down and lean forwards with my elbows on the table and my fingers clasped together, enjoying the subtle scent of his impatience.

"I was five," I say finally, "when I experienced my first transformation. So I figure I was born this way. And yes. Anna knew."

Charles raises his eyebrows. "Fascinating." He leans back in his chair. "What did she think when she first found out, I wonder?"

I meet his gaze. "She liked it. It turned her on."

A faint pink flush rises and fades in his cheeks, but his voice is even. "Go on."

I shrug.

"When she first saw me, I was a dingo. I'd been watching their camp for days. Working out what kind of people they were and why they were here. She was trying to collect water from an old well. Wasn't having much success, but she got the hang of it, eventually. The first thing I noticed was her red hair, the wind blowing it across her face. The second was her strong brown arms hauling up that bucket."

I pause for a moment to judge the effect of my words. His mouth is taut, his eyes giving nothing away.

"Maybe she felt me watching her, I don't know, but something made her turn around. She spotted me pretty quickly, and then, there we were, just staring at each other. For weeks

I'd watch her collect water in the afternoons. And she began to look out for me. I never came close though, never did anything, until one day she didn't come. I waited for her. The sun had started to set by the time she arrived, hurrying to the well. I could feel the change coming on me and I knew I had a choice, then and there, to let her see, or not. What decided me was the relief on her face when she spotted me. I stood facing her as the sun sank below the horizon. She saw me turn from a dingo to a man. She didn't budge. Didn't scream or cry out. Just stood there with this look on her face, as though she was watching the most beautiful thing in the world."

I stop and sit back, folding my arms.

Charles breathes in and out slowly in a kind of sigh.

"Well," he says softly, "Anna always was a rare one. Curious about things she shouldn't be."

He pours us some wine. I watch it swirling into the glasses and find I have no more words for him as I take a sip. Memories of Anna are swelling and bursting, bruising me from inside my ribcage.

"Her mother was the same." Charles's voice is a whisper and I almost think he's talking to himself.

He looks at me from above the rim of his glass as if weighing something. My eyes are feeling heavy and I hope that he'll leave whatever it is alone and let me get back to Freya and to sleep.

"I can't say I'm truly unhappy to do this to you Gardner, but I know Anna would not have it, so that causes me some small amount of consternation. If there's anything else you can tell me about yourself, it would help, if only to make it easier for my research team."

I frown, but the muscles in my face don't seem to want to respond. I try to meet his eyes, to work out what exactly he's just said, but his face looks distorted, as though I'm looking at him through a fishbowl. I slump in the chair and close my eyes. Time expands so that it takes an age for my eyelids to meet. My heart beats like a kettledrum, a deep, slow pounding in my ears. The world darkens and my last words stretch from me in glutinous pulses:

"You...b a s t a r d."

21

ANNA

*H*is words hit me like a brand of fire in my chest. "Gardner!"

By the time Lin reaches me, I'm sitting on the edge of her spare bed, shaking and whimpering. She tries to hold me, but I struggle and beat at her, pushing her away so that I can keep hold of the image blooming in my mind.

Gardner is lying on his side on some kind of metal table, naked, his eyes closed, with thick chains around his wrists and ankles. I try to focus on his face and the picture sharpens with my effort. There: the plane of his cheeks, rough with stubble; that single dark freckle just below the black fan of his eyelashes; a dark lock of hair across his forehead, lifting minutely in a faint breeze. I stare, uncomprehending, until, like a splash of water in my face, I realise I'm not looking at a static image, but a living vision. A new wash of panic sends me veering up and away from him.

"Steady Anna." I feel Lin taking a firm hold of my wrist. "Stay with it."

I breathe in and out, and try, tentatively, to turn from

Gardner to the surroundings. Immediately, the room begins to swim. I slow my turning and eventually the image crystalises again. The room is round, the inside of a pod, with wide threads of photosyn veins running up each wall and across the ceiling, creating so much light that there are no shadows. A curved table against one wall is filled with an assortment of metal objects: some small silver boxes, a wide-bladed knife, and a weapon that looks like an ECD. I spin around again and stop with a lurch. After another moment's lag, the room catches up so that I'm facing an oval window open to a predawn sky. I shoot up towards the roof.

"Breathe more slowly!" comes Lin's command in my ear. I force myself to take a slow, deep breath until I've settled into the room again above Gardner.

"Quickly!"

The voice is unfamiliar. A man wearing long brown gloves is holding open the door. His face is handsome in a kind of plastic, ageless way. Two others arrive; a man and a woman, both plainly attired, for Dome citizens. They hover in the doorway while the first strides across to Gardner, glitter cells in his tunic flashing under the bright photosyn. He tugs hard on each of the chains holding Gardner down.

"All clear. Come on, it's about to happen."

He switches off all the photosyn lighting, lifts the ECD from the table and hands the silver boxes to the other two. There's a tense silence while the sky turns from red to pink to orange. The gloved man trains the ECD on Gardner's torso and the others stand back with the silver boxes raised in front of them.

Finally, the first molten arc of the sun edges above the horizon. I look down at the familiar muscle and curve of Gardner's body as it melts and shifts until a dingo lies in the chains, eyes turned upwards under half-closed lids, tongue lolling out from between sharp, white teeth.

The tension in the room snaps and I feel myself shooting upwards as the people whoop and yammer all at once. I try to hold on but I can't; as though I've been free-diving and now a balloon has suddenly expanded, pulling me unrelentingly towards the surface.

I struggle and flail about, gasping for air. Lin is squatting before me in her nightgown, her hands upon my knees.

"Don't fight it. You're back. Take a breath."

I do, and the air surging in and out of my lungs calms me down a little. I look into Lin's dark eyes. She nods and stands up.

"You did well."

"Gardner..." My throat is hoarse.

She pours me a glass of water from a jug on the side table and passes it to me.

"That was a powerful amplifier I gave you."

"He needs me. I have to get to him!"

I try to get up, but my arms and legs seem to have turned to rubber.

"You need to rest."

"No!" I try again, but my body refuses to respond.

Lin places her hand on my shoulder. "Patience."

"You don't understand. Who knows what they're going to do—"

Lin interrupts me. "Who is doing this to your Gardner and where would you go to help him?"

"I..." I look down at my useless hands. "I don't know."

"Precisely. You need to sleep and eat and rest. And then you need to do more work."

"Just give me some more of that stuff. I'm ready now."

She shakes her head. "Only one dose in a twelve-hour period. Nobody can handle more."

"We don't have twelve hours!"

Lin shakes her head again, her gaze soft. "I'm sorry."

"Please Lin." Her face swims in my vision.

"No, Anna. You would die."

She watches me in silence as I cry, then she squats before me and brings my hands into her own.

"Does Freya not deserve her mother?"

I am defeated. On that hill again with my hands clawing into the earth and a floodlight on my family as they are carried away.

22

FAULK

One step in front of the other. That's what the fuckwits at the Academy would have said. The only sure way to go is to keep on going. Or some other such bilge. I've somehow found my way to the riverbank. It's still a plan, a way forward out of this nightmare. The River Gate beckons. And yet...

Her face, like a goddess on fire, the strength of her fight, the feel of hard muscle beneath soft skin. And her smell; salt and hot baked sand. I was nothing. A hollow, rotten log. Rubble and ruin. But she made me feel something. How can I leave that behind?

I walk well into the night. Anna Drake is burning me up. I think I see her, the flames of her hair always just ahead and around the corner. But it is nothing, no-one. A will-o'-the-wisp. I clench my fists as I walk, ferocious, desiring. And they all give me a wide birth—these hapless city worms.

If I were her dog, she'd want me. But I am her nothing. Her fucking piece of nothing.

I look for the moon, but it's nowhere to be seen, and the

grey stars ignore me, distant pin points with other agendas. I don't get tired from my walking, just stronger, angrier. Now I want to smash something, bash something. The next fucker I see is the next one down. Because this power has to go somewhere. Into soft flesh and splintering bone. I need to hear someone scream because then I won't be nothing. I'll be everything. Their death-dealing angel. All that there was in the end. But nobody passes me and the anger burns and fades to a sour stone in my stomach, leaving me sick with it.

I'm facing the dark heaving swell of the sea. I take off my shoes. The sand is cold as I walk towards the black mass of water and its luminous lip of froth teasing the shore. Anna, Anna. The waves and the shore, the waves and the shore.

The frigid seawater washes across my toes, and I can feel its acid tingle. I imagine her there, beneath the water. I'm holding her down and she is looking up at me, her hair floating out around her. She is a sorcerer and a terrorist, and I want her. Beneath me, beneath the waves.

A green light glows from under the water. One by one, luminescent jellyfish gather and blossom around my legs. I watch them, mesmerised by their undulating movements. They look aimless, slow, like they don't know what they're doing. But these lazy killers have it all worked out.

I walk further in, the cold constricting the blood in my legs and bringing me sharply into my body. Clarity returns in a silver wash. And I know I can be like that. Know that I'm still a hunter. Because what else is there, really? What else that means anything?

I don't sleep. I'm not tired. Adrenaline gets me back to Goldengass's compound. It's dark and quiet and the doors still respond to my thumbprint. I walk through the empty hallways, back to the velvet room, preparing myself for the stench of the dead guard. But it doesn't come. Someone has cleared it all up. The floor and walls gleam at me. The door to the velvet room is closed. I know I left it open. I turn the handle and push with a quiet swish.

All the lamps are on. Goldengass is sitting, calm as a king, with an old-fashioned gun trained on me. There's very little in me that cares if that thing blows. I walk up to him. Bang my fist against my chest.

"Do it, fucker. I don't care."

He looks genuinely startled and lowers his gun.

"What the hell, Parker?"

I stare him down. He gives in easily, flicking his weapon hand towards the chair to my left.

"Sit down will you, you're giving me a neck-ache."

I sit.

"So, that was a right cock-up, wasn't it?" Goldengass's tone is light. He's relieved. Relieved I'm here.

"Were you scared in the dark, sir?"

"Fuck you."

"Fuck yourself, sir."

"Parker, you're a mess."

He cradles the gun in his lap. I see the calculations in his eyes as he figures how to engage with this new level of madness. He wanted us grieving, angry, vengeful, subservient. That was our sweet spot, where we'd be the most use to him. He doesn't want this. This is too risky. I feel a belly laugh welling up from nowhere. To outwit Goldengass would be a beautiful thing. Something worth playing for. So I laugh like the madman he thinks I am until he shakes his head like a schoolteacher and sighs.

"Ah, I see…Anna Drake."

My laugh gets trapped in my throat.

His contempt is like thick, sour air I want to choke on, cough and spit out. Anything but breathe it in.

"What would you do to have her then, Parker? What would you like to do to her?"

The fight is draining from me, I can feel it, as something else wells up to take its place: dark visions of her that leave me weak. I clench my fists and my jaw and will myself not to break his gaze.

He laughs, soft and mean.

"As much of an abysmal failure as you are, Parker, you do keep me entertained."

As he shakes his head and wipes pretend tears from his eyes, the anger returns in me, red and hot, and all I can see is his round, shiny face and wet lips. I launch at him and smash that face to a pulp. Except that I don't. I sit like a volcano instead, waiting to hear all I need to know.

"All right then. The object of your...attention—" he stops, looking up like he's trying to remember something, "—now let me see." He grins, and I swear I can see feathers sticking out of his mouth. "No. Let's start at the beginning, shall we?" He inclines his head as though he's offering me a choice of boiled lollies.

"Start wherever the fuck you want."

He smiles, revelling in it. But as I simmer down and open my senses the way he trained me to, I look closely. And through the curtain of satisfaction and contempt, I can sense fear. I take that and store it away as he talks.

"Anna Drake. Daughter of the illustrious Charles Drake, inventor of the photosynthetic technology that powers our little climate-controlled corner of the world. Now what would we want with her, you're wondering?"

I watch him from under my brows. I'm already confused. She'd seemed such an outsider. So different to all the other city sheep. Goldengass continues.

"It seems she went rogue after high school. Skittered on

back to her mama, an Outdweller with the New Desert Alliance. Bunch of riff-raff and ideologues. They've always been a thorn in the side of Dome Protection. But recently we got wind of something bigger, and orders were to bring her and her child in. Simple. Right Parker?"

But I'm not looking at him anymore. I'd forgotten the child. Cut her out of the picture. A squirm of guilt churns in my stomach. I can see her now, holding up the ochre stone with big eyes, trying to be brave. *"Do you know where my daddy is?"* I snap back into the conversation, cutting across whatever he was about to say next.

"Why'd the girl ask about her dad?"

If Goldengass were a cat, his hair'd be standing on end right now. I can feel it in the electricity in the air and the shifty look in his eyes. I stand up. He goes for his gun, but I'm in and out like a snake, grabbing it before he can, holding it up in the air away from him.

"What are you not telling me?"

I almost mistake the fear in Goldengass's eyes. But it's not me he's afraid of.

"Talk."

"You don't want to know, Parker."

"Yes. I do."

He shakes his head, looks at me as though I'm a child. "Do you think she ever really wanted you?"

The trigger feels really good right now. I squeeze it a little. A frown flickers across Goldengass's face.

"All right. Put down the weapon, Faulk."

He's never called me by my first name before. Something about that intimacy gets to me. Says we've got a bigger enemy to face than each other. I lower the gun slowly and sit down.

"So, talk."

He takes a breath. "Her dad's the one who ripped out Crayman's jugular."

I shake my head. "But that was the dog."

Goldengass looks at me. "Yes, that was the dog."

"What the hell are you saying?"

He sighs. "The dog is only a dog half the time. The other half he's a man; the kid's dad, and your Anna's lover."

It doesn't make sense. I can't make it make sense. But the clenching in my gut tells me it's true. Anna never wanted me. It was all for her child. And then I get a flashback of the dingo's hot breath and its heavy paws on me. How it had sniffed at me before it'd howled and run off. Had it smelled her on me? With a rising chill, I realise how deep in shit I really am.

Goldengass is laughing now as he watches the expressions chasing each other across my face.

"Oh Parker, you are a fucked fool."

There's a roaring in my ears. I feel as though I'm sliding off the surface of something. Leftovers being scraped into a bin. And it is a cold, hard place to be. Any warmth I felt at the thought of Anna Drake drains out of me, and I'm left with nothing but bare steel.

"Tell me what to do."

His eyebrows flicker up in surprise as he takes in my face. Then he frowns, like he's considering.

"We have new orders. It's no longer a capture situation, for any of them."

New orders? It's the first time I've considered that Goldengass is not the head honcho here. That someone else might actually be calling the shots. Was that the fear I saw in him? Or is his fear the same as mine: Crayman's shocked face, a dingo's red teeth.

I nod. "I can do that."

He searches my eyes.

"What's their target?" I ask, to stop him from looking into me.

"The Dome itself."

I shake my head. "Shit."

"I'm glad you finally recognise the seriousn—"

"How?"

"Her girl's a weapon of some kind. That's all we know."

"The kid?"

"Yes, the kid." Goldengass's voice gets all short again as though he's had enough of questions, but I plough on.

"What about dog-man?"

Goldengass sighs. "As far as we know, he was with them as protector and guide."

"And because they're his family."

"Are you going to go soft on me again, Parker?"

I shake my head, breathe in and out to calm myself. "No, sir. But if we're going to work this thing, we need the entire picture." I stop short of pointing out how much I despise him for having kept me in the dark.

The child's face fills my mind again; brown skin, freckles over the bridge of her nose, her hair, red like her mother's, only darker. Darker because of her dad, probably. I want to see his face, to picture my enemy.

"What's he look like?"

Goldengass blinks. "Who?"

"The dad."

Goldengass leans across the side-table and pours himself a drink. I can feel him stalling, enjoying my impatience.

"I've not seen him."

"Any intel images?"

"Parker, if this has become a personal vendetta, then

you're of no use to me. If you have a death-wish, I can easily fulfil it for you now, in this room."

I look down, ready to explode. But he's not finished.

"It's possible they're on the run back home. I've got an entire squadron looking for them on the Outside. Your job is to make sure they're no longer with us in the Dome."

"Yes sir."

He squints at me, still suspicious.

"It's a termination, Parker. No hesitation. Anna Drake, the dog and the girl. Most especially the girl. Do you understand?"

I nod.

"Do you understand?"

"Yes, sir!"

~

I LEAVE the compound and head home. It seems an age ago I cut out my ID. What an idiot. What naïve dreams. The walk is good for me though, gets me feeling sharper, stronger.

My pod is just as I left it: drawers open, laying bare a thin layer of clothes collected on various field trips or saved from years ago when you could still buy them in shops. The rooms are bright and dusty in the late afternoon light. I look through the windows, searching out of habit. But there's no sign of the eagle today.

I sling off my pack. Tomorrow morning I'll re-pack with the simple items needed to carry out my task. And then it'll be over.

I open the pantry, pull out a dehydrated meal and pour it into a bowl, watching the desiccated carrots and peas fall in a dry, quiet flow. Mere husks of a life. I can't look. I go to switch on the kettle. Her cup sits on the bench top, a dark ring of coffee crusting the inside. A wave washes through my body: her mouth, her moisture, her pull. I can feel myself rehydrating with it, the blood rushing back into me. I slam my hand down hard to stop the flood with pain. But the pain is nothing. I grab the cup and throw it at the floor. The ceramic smashes. I walk out of the kitchen, crushing the pieces under my shoes. I bring up an interface for a business I've used before. On the lonelier nights.

She arrives at my door half an hour later. I'd requested red hair, but hers is short and straight. Her eyes are an unnatural blue, but then I guess they're back-lit. Her body feels real enough; soft with fat in all the right places, raised dark circles on her breasts, a smooth flat stomach and even a navel. After a while, though, none of it matters. I am lost in her perfect body, knowing I can neither hurt her nor be known to her, because she doesn't feel a thing.

23

ANNA

*S*hama?

I am dreaming. She is cradling me in her pouch lined with fur. There is a slit of light, a world too bright. She holds me with a female warmth and power, a musky strength of blood and skin, and does not let me go. We are moving. Up and down; a macropod canter. It is a rocking and a loving and it is all that I need.

Shama. Take me home now. Please take me home.

To the time before the bargain. The worst side of a lost deal. When all I had given my body to was the moon and a man with two faces, and the birth of a slippery wonder with bright eyes.

The slit lengthens. Lin's heavy curtain lets in a crack of Dome-muted sunlight. Not the outside. Just another kind of womb. Hapless, we devour, as the silkworms do; the leaf-greenness and the wholeness torn and chewed, the life sucked out and into ourselves. I shiver at what we will become once this devouring is done.

I try to remember. Find my way back. Freya. Our course

was set when she shivered to life beneath the diamond sky. Alchemical, lucid. Should have named her Aurora. Except that this was not the name she wanted. Even from inside me, she told me she was Freya. That she was her, and not me; not what *I* wanted, but what *she* needed to become. And Gardner and I had listened. Because we were the same as her, really. We were the ones to choose our own fate. Until now.

I sit up in Lin's spare bed, galvanised. *Gardner. Hold on, hold out for me. Today I will find you.*

⁓

GARDNER

There is cold beneath me. I ache but cannot move. Something shifts above me. Only a shimmer of something. I can feel it but I can't see it because my eyes are closed and I cannot open them. It is only breathing that I can do now. Breathing and shivering. I don't choose to breathe and shiver, but it is all my body will do.

The shimmer of something above me is like a rose in the desert. It is colour and warmth and water where there should be none. I would reach for it but I can't. It is with my heart that I hear it, not my ears. I cannot hear with my ears.

She is strength and fire. Stubbornness and delicacy. Thorns and velvet. And I know it's Anna. Can only be her.

Warmth floods me. I don't know if it's from me or from her.

And then it's gone. The cold returns and the chains cut and twist.

⁓

ANNA

Lin has me eat first. I don't taste the food. Just wash it down with water. I don't even jump as Zotzi swoops in to perch on the back of a chair and reaches out to devour the fruit Lin has cut and laid out in a bowl for him. I feel his gaze on me as I leave the room with my vial.

This time, the transition is easier. A floating downwards, feather-like.

I'm standing in a forest. No, not a forest—a plantation. Rows fan out in every direction. The trees are tall, with weeping, lacy canopies of bright, young leaves. The Silk Forest. A place so closely guarded, so hidden and protected that it's almost myth. But with mulberry trees as far as I can see, enough to feed the Dome-maker silkworms forever, this cannot be any other place.

Taking a step is easy, almost as though I'm solid. So I take another, and another. At every tree, there is a choice, a path I could take. But I walk straight ahead, trusting that I'm moving closer to where I need to be.

Soon I reach the heart of the plantation: a round, clear centre of grass, ringed with trees who lean in towards the light as though they would march forward to fill the gap if they could. In my journey to the heart, I seem to have moved through the seasons, as here the branches are laden with deep red jewels; mulberries hanging in their hundreds below rough-edged leaves.

I stand at the edge of the circle, waiting. Sunlight, always sunlight. It angles in; golden. A faint breeze rustles through the trees, whisper to whisper, song to song, as though the trees are waiting too.

And then I see him: Gardner, standing across the clearing, bathed in yellow light; not a dingo, but a man under the sun's bright gaze. My heart, for I seem to have one in this most corporeal of visions, begins a loud tattoo. He is so known to me, old and yet always new. In the daylight, his angles seem sharper, his body stronger. Even though I know it's not his body. Perhaps not even him. And this last thought brings blood roaring to my ears.

"Gardner?"

"Anna." He sounds relieved, and I see that I'm a vision to him too.

We walk towards each other, from the edge to the centre, and it's as though we are meeting for the first time. We reach for each other. He draws me to him so that my cheek rests against his chest. The solid press of his body and his smell of earth and sun-baked rocks feels familiar and real.

Then he takes hold of my arms, draws me away a little so that he can see me.

"How, Anna? How are we here?"

I don't want to break the spell. This cocooned centre. But there's worry on his face and there is Freya.

"I'm with Dr Kuanyin. She's helping me find you."

There's a tightness around his eyes, a distance I take for wariness. He looks down at his body; human, not canine.

"That explains this."

I feel the urgency return. "Tell me—I need to know where you are. Where Freya is."

He presses my hand. "We're at your father's. I'm not safe. He drugged Freya. Us both."

A wave of horror washes through me, hot and cold to my stomach.

"At the Night Market? Was it *him*?"

Gardner shakes his head. "I don't know. That was Dome Protection. But he might have been pulling the strings."

"So, how—"

"We escaped. Left the Dome. Went to Meiying and Renshu."

"But you came back?!"

"Yes."

"Why?"

"For you."

A heavy stone drops into my heart. Guilt and grief push me to the ground. He kneels beside me.

"Anna—"

I shake my head. "You don't know what I've done."

"Yes. I do."

I look up at him. Pain is printed in the blue of his eyes. He can't hold that from me, or the anger, the grief.

"I'm coming for you," I say. Because it's all I *can* say.

He gets to his feet. "I hope so."

He turns and walks away from me across the clearing.

"Gardner!" My words fight with the white rustle of leaves as the breeze shivers through the trees, and I'm not sure whether he has heard me. "Please wait for me!"

He turns around, and for a moment, holds my gaze. Then, like a rush of river water through broken ice, he melts into a dingo and races off amongst the trees.

I'm not pulled to the surface like last time. Instead, I remain sitting in the green heart of the city, trying to make sense of my father's deception, to unravel the truth from his lies, with Gardner's absence like an aching hole in my side. My body warms with impatience, but the languorous forest around me seems to hold me down. *Wait*, it says. *Not yet.* Leaves shift and sigh around me, but I hear no other sounds. No birdsong. As I run my hand across the short, green lawn, it occurs to me that there are no ants or other small crawling things either amongst the intact, green blades; all has been turned to sterile treasure; gold under an eternal sun. It is a place so unlike my mother's home, where, far from the Midas-touch of humanity, the long yellow grass and sloughing eucalypts hum with life.

Only the vein of the river brings insolent life into this city. Life that would harbour itself amongst us. I can just remember a time when this riparian cargo of snakes and possums, greenhoods and daisy-bushes, was cherished, nurtured, valued; when the Dome was a place of sanctuary. Back then, it shone like a beacon of safety, of possibility. There were so many who sought entrance to the Great Southern Silk Dome after the Retreat, whose rank and colourful camps blossomed at the borders, determined that exile should not be their lot; that they, too, deserved a place in the golden metropolis. Hopeful at first and eventually angry and rife with disease, this patchwork of people gradually became more vocal, more daring in their desperation.

And then came the crackdown: the erasure of all who threatened the safety of humanity's treasured elite. Dome Protection's actions over those three fateful days elevated them to a far loftier position of power than their original mandate had provided them. Their atrocity was also the act that forced my mother's hand, that awakened the wife of Charles Drake to the awareness that she could no longer pretend not to see. That she must take their little girl, return to the Outdwellers; to her aunts, who had helped birth her child and who were the only family she knew. That this time, she must leave the Dome for good.

I lie in the grass, lift my arm across my eyes to shield them from the brightness and from the memories, vague and nightmarish, of our flight, of what we saw as we ventured beyond the border of all I'd ever known. I'd been younger than Freya, to be sure. But the experiences of some things soak into you bone deep, without full remembering. And my body and heart have never forgotten...

Why am I not back with Lin? I try to imagine myself floating upwards and into her room, but nothing shifts. The breeze turns cold against my skin. I uncover my face. The sunlight has gone and black clouds swirl, building, filling the sky as I watch. I try to get to my feet, but something pushes down on my chest, a weight like that of a sleeping cat, just heavy enough to keep me lying there and staring into the fast-bruising sky. Then I hear her—Shama—and she sounds like thunder.

Anna, beware!

In the cloud, a familiar face forms: Faulk, with eyes like an angry green sea, crooked nose and the closed, uneven line of his lips, radiating enmity. I draw in a sharp breath.

Then a bewildering sequence of images follows, with flashes of time speeding up and slowing down. I see glowing jellyfish, Faulk baring his teeth, the taut grip of a weapon in both his hands; a white cup shattering, ceramic pieces bouncing slowly upwards and then quickly crashing down. Faulk's brown hands around a smooth white waist; a woman with a pale, expressionless face, electric blue eyes and short red hair; Faulk cleaning his weapon, stowing it in his pack; standing by a window, searching the sky. With a retina-burning flash, the images vanish and the cloud disgorges a torrent of rain. I watch it hammering the Dome roof and sliding down the sides like tears.

I close my eyes, no longer knowing if I'll return. Shama's voice is so faint now and I can hardly hear her. Or was it my voice all along? *My mother says an early child is a lucky child because she carries a few spare days to use at the end of her life.* Extra days, extra days to use at the end. Now I know I will need them.

"Lin!" My voice is a ghost's voice. No volume, no resonance. "Lin!"

It is Freya's name I call now. She is little and running with skinny brown legs that have just learnt how to. A funny tiptoe run. Gardner and I are laughing. I've put her hair up into two high bunches and she looks like a tiny fox-girl, her face alive with delight, laughing with the pure pleasure of running. My heart is full and sore with her vulnerability and trust. All I want is to hold her. To kiss her. To hope that the light will never leave her face.

I OPEN MY EYES, and my face is wet. I'm lying on my back on the floor of Lin's spare bedroom. I sit up, shaking all over. I take several tries to stand up, splaying my legs like a newborn antelope. When I finally make it upright, I reach out for the bedframe. As I clutch at it, my hand touches something warm. It moves, and I let out a shriek. Zotzi jumps and flaps up to the roof, clinging on to a beam and looking down at me, his body quivering.

"Sorry, Zotzi! I'm sorry. You startled me, that's all."

He eyes me. I look up at him, trying to relax my face into a friendly smile.

Eventually, he flutters down onto the bed. I reach out and he shuffles forwards on his wings like elbows and takes a tentative sniff of my hand.

"You okay?"

He looks at me with big dark eyes and then turns towards the window. A tangle of shrubs and trees in front of a high fence obscures much of what must be sunset from us. The deep red of the sky sends a shiver through me. I have lost a whole day and Gardner will be changing now. I wonder whether they're watching him or doing more than watching as he shifts back into a man tied to his metal operating table. I go to leave, but a movement at the window makes me turn around.

"Zotzi?"

The small, dark-furred creature is lengthening, shifting and blurring in front of me. I gasp. I'd forgotten. Although I've seen Gardner transform so many times, it's a shock to see it happening to someone else. With a last stretch, a young boy stands before me, silhouetted against the twilight.

He scampers towards the sliding door behind me and tries to widen the crack he must have snuck in through to get into the room. It's too heavy for him to move, though, and he turns to face me. Now I can see that he's only a little older than Freya, with a mane of tightly curled black hair and bright blue eyes that are eerily similar to Gardner's. I catch myself staring, grab the quilt off the foot of the bed and walk carefully towards him.

"Here, you don't want to get cold."

He allows me to wrap it around his shoulders.

"Shall we go and see Lin?"

He nods and I slide open the door for us.

"WE CAN MAKE A PLAN NOW, but then you must get some sleep."

I shake my head, but Lin's eyes are stern, her small mouth set.

"You must. Your visions have weakened you. You need rest if you're to be of any use to your family."

Lin sets down bowls of clear soup and some bread in

front of me and Zotzi. He has been watching us keenly but hasn't uttered a word. She gives him a kind smile.

"Eat up my dear."

Then she sits down with her own bowl, breaks up the bread and dips it neatly into her soup.

After a few mouthfuls, she looks hard at me. I sigh and pick up my spoon.

We eat in silence until Lin turns to Zotzi.

"Would you like to help Ms Drake?"

Zotzi glances up from his soup and nods quickly, his eyes flicking to me and then back to Lin.

"Zotzi will help you find Gardner. Would you like to tell her your special trick, Zotzi?"

He nods again and then speaks some soft, lilting words: "I can paint pictures with my voice."

I raise my eyebrows.

Lin smiles. "A skill otherwise known as echolocation. He can create a sound map of your father's building for you, sort of like an x-ray image, so that you can pinpoint exactly where in it Gardner is being held."

"Goodness! That's brilliant Zotzi."

He gives me a broad, proud smile.

"Another reason to wait until tomorrow morning then, when Zotzi will be in the right modality to perform the task."

"All right," I say, and as I concede, I find myself longing for bed.

24

FAULK

*T*hey allow a sprinkle of yesterday's rain to filter through during the night. It's just after dawn when I venture out, my pack light with only weapons and some water. The air is humid and the street, black with moisture. A sparrow perching in the tangled jasmine at the base of my pod puffs and shakes its feathers amongst the wet leaves. The rain has brought throbbing life to the city; I can feel it in my body. It's a strange day for killing.

I walk towards the sea, this time with purpose. On the road beside the beach I am passed by a golden car, its top half open to the air like a gaudy float, its passengers with laughing faces and shimmering skin; bright creatures, high on Joy. They don't see me. Or the seagull swooping low in front of them. It hits the front of their vehicle, bounces and rolls across the road behind them as they drive on and away, heedless, and comes to rest in the gutter beside me; its head twisted, blood blooming like a red flower across its breast.

I pick it up. I don't know why. Take it and bury it beneath the yellow sand, my heart pumping with the defiance of the living. There's blood on my fingers. I wipe it on my forehead. A talisman. So that she knows—my gentle gatherer, patient angel—knows that I am giving her three more souls today. Anna's face, with her watching eyes, swims in my vision. The familiar awakening rush from the base of my spine spreads throughout my body. But today it is spiced with the nearness of her death. The prospect of stilling her singing blood is my drug today, not quite Joy; something with more bass notes; a deeper, velvet drink, potent and electric.

I reach the pod-tree of the illustrious Charles Drake. It's a flamboyant construction, thick with veins and hung with white pods in a nautilus spiral up the stem. The top pods, according to Goldengass, belong to the man himself, and the lower pods are the holdings of Drake Industries.

I scout the street outside, looking for the best spot to conceal myself. A high stone wall diagonally opposite, hedged in by a spreading fig tree, provides an obliging structure. I begin by climbing the wall into the fig's branches to see if I can look into any of the pods. High amongst the dense foliage of the smaller branches, I find myself level with the lowest pod. Unfortunately, its windows are mirror glass. I climb down to a concealed fork of wide grey limbs and open my pack. My handgun is a cold weight. I'm thankful the distance is short and that it's all I'll need. I settle in for the wait.

The day lengthens. My body has long ceased to feel the soreness in my muscles. Numbness enfolds me from the inside out. The morning shifts to grey with the sun hidden behind a bank of clouds; another rainstorm building beyond the Dome.

Goldengass had been so sure she'd come. They've had her dog-man and her girl in there for over twenty-four hours. She must know where they are by now. Although, now I think of it, why should she? None of them have active trackers or even headsets.

I call him up. His face wobbles to life in front of me.

"You got it wrong. She's not coming."

Goldengass frowns. "What are you talking about?"

"I mean, you got your intel wrong. She's not here."

"She's on her way Parker."

"And how's she supposed to know where they are?"

"We saw her heading to Drake's just after dawn. She's been circling the place at a distance for hours."

"What's keeping her?"

"We don't know. But she's closing in."

I eye him for a moment. "All right."

"Patience, Parker. We want this done right."

I switch off the interface.

The heavy sky brings cover, so I climb out of the branches to stretch for a bit, hidden in the gloom between the tree and the wall. Then I hear a noise and back myself up against the tree, readying my pistol with a quiet click.

I haven't got time to climb the tree again and I curse myself for my miscalculation. I peer around the trunk. A flame of red hair is visible through the hanging foliage. Anna. She's striding towards her father's building. In a moment, she'll be standing at the glass reception door. Ten metres, eight metres, four. She stops. Her back is not square to me, but she's angled to the right and I easily target her heart, my finger resting lightly on the trigger. Blood thuds in my ears. I take a breath, anchor myself for the kickback and steady my aim.

Then I see my angel: a black, winged beast alighting on her shoulder. Not pretty at all, not like the last time. This one is straight from hell. It sniffs at the air, opens its mouth in a silent scream, and turns towards where I'm hidden. Black eyes stare straight at me, as though the foliage between us is nothing but cellophane. Anna turns too, her body suddenly tensed, her face a question.

I fire.

The shot knocks me back against the tree and leaves my ears buzzing. When I look again, she's on her knees and the beast is flying towards me, already so close I can hear the beating of its leathery wings. I grab my pack with shaking hands and somehow find my way back along the wall. As soon as I hit the street, I run. Run along the beachside path, up the main road and into the brightness of the city.

Finally, I reach my pod, slam the door behind me, and make damn sure it's locked.

"Fuck, fuck, fuck."

It saw me. Knew who I was. This time, death noticed *me*.

25

ANNA

I'm on my knees before the pain registers. Then I feel it: a searing sensation in my shoulder and the nauseating realisation that my body has been breached. I reach my hand to the wound and it comes away bloody. I twist around to assess the damage but can't quite see it. Then my world funnels to black.

When I open my eyes, it is to a vaguely familiar face.

"Hi love. You're back with us."

White ringlets brush my cheek. They frame the soft features of a woman with pale blue eyes. I search for her name.

"Sirena?"

"That's me." She smiles and holds my wrist.

I try to bring saliva back into my mouth to unstick my dry tongue. "I thought you were a tailor."

"Tailor, medic. Anything your father needs really."

I go to speak again, but she shakes her head and puts a finger to her lips. A timer flickers in front of her as she takes my pulse.

"Sixty-seven," she says, and the interface disappears. "Good," she meets my eyes and smiles, and then answers my unasked question. "The bullet that lodged itself into the wall of Reception grazed your shoulder. A lucky miss. Your father's tracking down the weapon number as we speak. Can't have people going around hurting his daughter now, can we?"

"What about his granddaughter? Or his son-in-law?" My voice cracks as I try to raise it above a dry whisper.

Sirena holds up her hands. "Calm, Ms Drake. All in good time. For now, you need to recover."

I sit up, yank at some tube in my arm and immediately regret it. The resulting dizziness threatens to black me out again. Sirena catches me, stopping me from falling sideways, and guides my head back onto the pillow. Then she raises the front of the bed so I'm sitting supported against it.

"That better?"

I nod.

"Now, another of my various roles over the last couple of days has been that of nanny."

I stare at her uncomprehendingly.

"Your Freya is here, and she is well."

My heart feels as though it's swelling to the size of a balloon.

"Let me see her!"

Sirena raises a hand. "We're just waiting on your infection risk status to come back clean and then I'll bring her to you myself."

"When will that be?"

Sirena's smile warms her eyes. "I think we'll hurry it up, don't you?"

I gulp in great lungfuls of air as my heart races in anticipation. "When?"

"Within the hour."

The tears come as a surprise after so much waiting.

She hands me a soft cloth and I wipe my face, trying to find some control amidst the turmoil of my mind. I look at Sirena through the blur.

"And I'll need to see my father."

"Of course. He wants to see you too."

"As soon as possible." Even I am surprised by the hardness of my voice.

Sirena studies my face. "I'll go now and make you something nice to wear."

I protest, but she shakes her head. "Trust me. I find it's always best to meet a man on one's own terms. Particularly such a man as your father."

I look down at my body: hooked up, prostrate, my clothes bloody and torn.

She watches me and her gaze holds more steel than I had credited her with. "You won't regret it."

I allow myself a small nod.

"Good, I'll be back soon."

WHEN SIRENA RETURNS, she unhooks the catheter and dabs some clear ointment over the puncture mark, then helps me to stand.

"How does that feel?"

There's no dizziness this time. "Better."

"You're clear of any infection. Just keep the shoulder wound covered for the next 24 hours. You seem to be responding well to the stem cells and we've applied a nano-accelerant so you shouldn't really need more time than that."

She reaches behind her. "And more enjoyably, here's your outfit."

She lays the clothes on the bed in front of me. She has created a two-piece outfit in typical New Desert style. The leggings are dark grey, tough and flexible, soft and light, and the top is a blue, woven brocade, a cotton mimic, with a broad cape hood. The only concession to the city is the glimmer cells woven throughout the fabric.

"Sirena…" I find tears threatening again.

"I thought you'd like it." She beams.

I cross my arms. "No tracker this time though?"

She raises her eyebrows. "I've installed an interfacer for you. It's only Dome-local. Longer-range ones need authentication from your father. It's in your left sleeve."

"Thank you."

"You're most welcome. Now, Charles is on his way to see you."

"What about my daughter?"

Sirena meets my gaze. "He's requested that he speak to you first."

"No. I need to see her now."

Sirena stands to block the doorway. "I will bring her to you. I promise. It's just…it's not worth my while to disobey your father. Perhaps you know the feeling."

I will myself to breathe. "Only too well."

"All right then. I'll let you get changed."

She bows out of the room.

It feels as though an hour has passed by the time I hear a soft knock at the door. I stand up, my new clothes comforting and strengthening me, holding me within my mother's world. Then I sit down again, not wanting to be caught standing at attention.

"Come in."

He enters the room, stiff-backed, and quietly closes the door behind him. I'm struck by how familiar his carefully neutral expression is to me, and I'm unnerved by my bodily response, my childish desire to have him hold me in his arms. I breathe; breathe and think of Gardner.

"Anna." His voice is scolding, as though I'm fifteen and have stayed out too late.

"What have you done to Gardner?"

"I could have helped you. Why leave?"

"Gardner. What have you done to Gardner?"

A long muscle tightens beneath his cheekbones.

"Your dog?" He raises his eyebrows, but his eyes remain cold. "Why, Anna?"

"No, Charles. I'm asking the questions."

He stares at me; a pale statue of man. Then he lunges forward and grabs my wounded arm.

"You made a mockery of me," he hisses in my ear. "You thought to hide the fact that you were sleeping with a dog. A freak. What were you thinking? Was it to spite me? To choose this...this thing. To have a child to it!"

A throbbing pain begins in my wound. I meet his ferocious gaze, my mouth clamped shut to prevent nausea from overwhelming me. Our eyes lock and I can feel a battle being played out between us, word for word, cut for cut.

Eventually, he lets go, blinks and looks down his straight nose at me, his nostrils flaring. "Why?"

"Why do you think?!"

"I don't—"

"You've never known how to love something that doesn't fit within your safe, tightly controlled world. That's why my mother left you. You tried to contain her wildness, couldn't accept she might have different ideas to yours. Might love something that you didn't understand!"

I almost flinch at the look in his eyes, sure he's going to hit me. But his voice is quiet with venom and pain.

"Is this what you really believe?"

"Yes."

"How little you know of your mother."

"Don't even try that."

"All wars have two sides."

"And that's your problem. You think everything is a battle."

"Your mother is the one who planted these radical ideas in your mind."

"Radical! Is that what you call them? My mother is the only one of the two of you who ever sought to give me any understanding, any kind of intellectual commentary or analytical tools to examine this fucked-up world we've created. The world *you* so nobly helped to create."

He stares at me.

My throat is sore from shouting.

"And from which you have benefitted richly." He spits out the words with cold precision. "No matter how much of an outsider you pretend to be, Anna, you are as much a product of this world as I am. Your life is supported by the lives that were forfeited for your privilege. At least I am not squandering my advantages. You and that half-man, all of it—I see it so clearly now—is an elaborate attempt to rebel against me, to forget the blood on your own hands."

My palms feel hot and slick with sweat. I cannot speak because it is true. Because part of it is true. True enough for me to feel the breath-sucking blow of his words hitting my stomach as though they were real fists.

And yet, a part of it, surely, is not true. Gardner. I love him for more than this. Don't I? For more than rebellion's sake alone. I reach for that, grasp it and clasp it to me because I must. Because Gardner is here, and that is why I came.

"Give him back to me. And bring me back my child. We shall leave and not return. Then you'll never need to think about us again. I'll be dead to you and the shame you feel at having such a daughter will no longer trouble you."

"I'm afraid I can't do that Anna."

"Why not?"

"Because you are more precious to me than you suppose."

"*Precious?!* Precious as a daughter or precious like your money?"

He shrugs. "Both."

"Then if you care for me, give me what *I* most care for."

"And what is that?"

"My daughter and her father!"

"What if I could give you more than that?"

"There is no more than that."

He tilts his head to the side. "But there is."

"What?"

"A key. A key to how we might live the life we've all been seeking. A way to live, to thrive, outside the Dome."

I snort. "My mother already does that perfectly well."

"Underground," he sniffs, "like a troglodyte. That is not what I call thriving."

I stare at him.

"You are interested. Despite yourself. Think how this would help you, you and your...family." He wrinkles his nose.

I look away from him, the blood rising to my ears so that I am almost deaf with it. He continues, heedless.

"I've been carrying out some new research. Looking at how we might power our lives from within our own bodies."

"We already do that. It's called eating food."

"Don't be facetious Anna; it doesn't suit you. No, I'm working on incorporating photosynthetic technology into the human organism. It would power our communications, our digital technologies, our light sources. We could create personal climate-controlled fields so that we can be free again, free to be in the world as we were meant to be!"

The old fervour in his voice slingshots me back to my childhood, to the days when he and my mother would talk for hours together while I played at their feet, ignored as they stoked the passion of their ideas.

"And what does this have to do with me?"

"I want you to stay here with me, Anna. Freya can stay, too. I've nothing against her. She didn't ask to be born to a—" he pauses, takes a breath. "I miss you. I miss family. You could help me, help change the world you so despise. Change it into something better."

"And what about Gardner?"

"Anna, come on. How much do you love him really? I understand—he's symbolic to you. Important, in that way. But you're a grown woman now. Not a young girl trying to show the world how different she can be."

I speak quietly and clearly. "You're wrong. That is not how I see him."

His upper lip curls. "You have more of me in you than you will admit. I recognised it in you as a child and I see it in you now. Who else would have the gumption to waltz up to the Great Southern Dome, gain entry as you did, and remain a free woman?"

"But I am not a free woman."

He sits down on a chair next to me.

"Yet, in my home you are safe."

"Father—"

"Consider it, Anna. Please."

"Let me see him."

He sighs heavily. "Get some sleep. Tomorrow he has to go. I will release him beyond the borders of the city. He'll remain unharmed by me. I give you my word."

A hollow pit forms where my heart should be.

"Let me see him and I'll consider your proposal."

He stands up, presses his lips together and gives me a curt nod. "That's my girl."

As I wait, I sleep and dream. Shama is walking towards me through a thin veil of mist, and in her hands she holds a nest of woven twigs. The air is thick with moisture, and weak sunlight angles into the green around us. Branches hung with pendant mosses criss-cross above our heads and filmy ferns clasp the rough base of a tree fern trunk beside me. Shama places the nest into my cupped hands. It feels so light. I run my fingers across its intricate tracery, stroke the soft moss and feathers within it. The more I hold it in my hands, the more it feels like a living thing; I can almost feel its heart beating against my palms. I look up at Shama. She nods once and then steps back into the mist. I hold the nest, its warmth spreading from my fingers into every part of me. And with the warmth comes a heaviness, until the nest feels like such a weight in my hands that I almost can't carry it anymore.

Shama? Shama!

I wake up calling her name. My face is damp, and the room is dark. There is a soft knock at the door. It opens a little and I see Sirena, her face illuminated by the bioluminescent dress she is wearing. I sit up.

"I'm awake."

She opens the door fully and enters.

"I wasn't sure," she says quietly and perches on the end of the bed. "How does your arm feel?"

I move my shoulder around a bit. "Better. It doesn't hurt."

She smiles, her teeth glowing. "Good. I was going to bring Freya to you, but she's asleep now. Would you like to wait until morning?"

"No! I want to see her now. But don't wake her."

Sirena nods and stands up. "Okay. Follow me."

We pad through a honeycomb of rooms before she stops in front of a closed door with a small internal window. I peer through into a rounded room lit by a soft, yellow night lamp. She is lying asleep on a small bed, her hands tucked beneath her chin, her dark copper hair like a nest of autumn leaves around her face. I suck in a sharp breath and my eyes fill with water.

"Let me in."

Sirena unlocks the door. I tiptoe into the room and sit next to Freya on the bed. I touch her cheek. It is soft and warm. Her breathing pauses briefly and her mouth opens and closes. I lie down beside her, move in to the curve of her back, and carefully, so as not to wake her, place my arm across her. I close my eyes and breathe her in.

Eventually, Sirena whispers from the doorway.

"Charles has sent through a message. He says you may look in on Gardner now." She places a kind hand on my arm. "You won't be able to wake him, of course."

The click of the lock to Freya's room feels loud. I follow Sirena in silence, my body a hollow ache for my daughter's sleeping warmth.

26

FAULK

The fox is soft under my hands, her red coat sparked with brass in the sunlight. I stroke her and she's like silk under my fingers. I try to pick her up, hold her to me, but she snarls, kicks her clawed hind limbs into my stomach and bounds out of my lap.

I look for Anna's ghost amongst the treasure dancers on my shelf. She's not there. Not there and I know why. I offered her up, but death chose me instead.

My blinds are closed against the sunset, I crouch in the dark. I will stay here forever with visions swarming through me.

Except that I need to pee.

I drag myself to the bathroom and stand in the dark, releasing a hot stream into the bowl. Its acrid tang works like smelling salts, forcing me out of my stupor. At the wash-basin, I turn my hands over and over in the warm water, unable to meet my own eyes in the mirror. My job is not done.

I grab my pack and slide out into the twilight. The sky is

a clear indigo, and the city, a quiet, distant throb. All around me is silence. I walk, seeing foxes in every shadow.

Soon I'm beneath the ancient fig. Charles Drake's pod tree looks as though it will float away tonight, just a bunch of moons on strings. Guards stand, silhouetted, in a ring around the entrance building. I don't intend to get inside with Drake Industries on alert. It's hours yet until morning, plenty of time. I study the guards' attire, their manner and weaponry through my scope until I have it down to the finest detail. Then I take a photo and send it through to my printer. I'll have time to collect my clothes and weapons and return in full Drake Industries regalia before sunrise.

THE SKY IS a luminous predawn as I hurry back to the fig tree, the dark blue Drake Industries uniform stiff against my skin. With everyone's features shifting and shimmering in the half-light, it is a little thing to meld into the watch ring around the building. A grunt of relief is all I receive as I whisper to my chosen guard that his shift is over and it's my turn to take his place.

We wait and a quiet half hour passes. The rising sun's first fiery rays make us all blink and we watch in contained and solitary rapture as the sky ripens from pink to gold to a tentative new blue.

It seems I was a little ahead of the wave, as only now do the rest of the guards arrive to relieve the night-guards. One replacement; a dark-haired young man with light hazel, almost golden eyes walks up to me. I shake my head.

"No need, I'm fresh in."

He looks as though he's about to query me, but at that instant, the doors slide open. He finds a spot a few metres from me and stands to attention. I take up the stance too, my eyes on the entrance, hoping his curiosity will be short-lived.

The procession that files out of the building is the strangest I've seen. Charles Drake himself is at its head, arm in arm with his stone-faced daughter. Anna's hair has been braided into an elaborate bundle on her head and she's dressed in New Desert style. A twang of something like to nostalgia shivers through me as I think back to the simplicity of following her and her family through the desert, the routine of tracking and camping, following their traces, foe upon foe.

She looks pale, but healed from my bullet wound. Another wave washes through me, this time of profound relief. I allow myself to feel into the paradoxical satisfaction of seeing her alive. Like the fish you just can't get out of your mind, the one you have to keep catching and releasing, catching and releasing until the day comes, maybe for no particular reason, or maybe because you want your life back, that you go out there and you catch it for good.

Following Charles and his daughter is a group of men and women in Drake Industries attire. Theirs is a different uniform to the guards', with a logo just above their hearts of a photosyn vein coiled around a white sun. I figure they're from R&D. The man in the lead has long brown gloves and an angular face. Behind him is a cage hovering just above the ground, being propelled invisibly forwards, with two people on either side carrying ECDs. Inside the cage is the dingo, sprawled on the metal floor, out cold.

All but two of the guards slip into formation behind them. I step into line too, my movements only a fraction out of step as I imitate the guards closest to me. Thankfully, we don't march, only walk fast enough to catch up with the lead of the train and form a flanking guard. I'm positioned behind and to the left of Anna, just out of her view, but close enough that I can see the back of her neck.

After a few minutes, we turn onto the beach road. A platoon of cars is waiting for us. Charles and Anna step into the first one with the front two guards. The cage is locked onto an open tray behind them and the rest of us fill up the successive cars. I sit by a window with the golden-eyed sentry and two other guards from the patrol wedged against me, and look out across the bay. The water is still and glassy. I count the minutes silently, until finally we begin to move off in the direction of the North Gate.

Thankfully, nobody speaks for quite a while.

Eventually, the guard at the opposite window wordlessly offers us mints from his pocket, but only the man sitting next to him takes one with a nod.

"No, thanks," says gold-eyes. I'm surprised at how young he sounds. Out of the edge of my vision, I can see he's trying to maintain his upright posture as the car swerves around the bends along the shore.

"Drake's girl," offers the second guard slowly around his mint. "She's a bit of all right."

The first guard sniggers. Gold-eyes turns to them but says nothing. I can feel the blood rising to my face.

"What'ya reckon Yuke? Would you go her?" Gold-eyes, aka Yuke, turns to the road ahead, his back straight.

The first guard laughs. "Too old for Yuke I reckon. Hear she's a mum."

"I dunno, a bit of experience'd do him good."

I turn from the window to see Yuke's blanched face turn a bright pink.

"Eh? Whaddya reckon?" the second guard lands a meaty hand on Yuke's stiff shoulder. He ignores it.

They both start laughing now.

"Red-heads give the best—"

"Cut it out." I've growled out the words before I can think better of it.

They both shoot surprised looks at me, as though they hadn't realised I was there.

Yuke avoids everyone's eyes.

"What's your problem?" says the second guard.

"No problem," I say.

"I think he's got a problem," says the first guard.

"Leave it alone," pipes up Yuke.

"Oh sweetheart, ain't you a saint," says the first guard as the second one reaches across Yuke to grab my shirt.

"What's your problem?" he hisses into my face.

I whip an arm up and grab him around the back of the neck, pressing in at two pressure points. He goes as limp as a kitten. I press harder and he howls with pain.

"What the fuck?!" shouts the other guard.

"I told you. I've got no problem," I say quietly, shoving my assailant back into his seat over a cowering Yuke.

I turn back to face the window, quietly steadying my breathing.

We reach the North Gate tunnel in silence. As my anger ebbs away, I realise what an idiot I've been to bring attention to myself. It's not so much the sense of unfinished business from the guards that has me concerned, but the possibility that Yuke will decide to stick to me in some misguided notion he's found himself a buddy. I look out into the dark tunnel and refocus on my reflection. I can see the guards reflected too, staring ahead, the energy in the car shifting, bringing me hope that their professionalism will kick back in when we're finally out of the car.

We pass beneath the arching pillars of the North Gate with a shadow, flash, shadow, flash, until we're out the other side. I imagine they won't want to range too far from the Dome and risk losing the benefit of their photosyn tech. The downside of a living in a cocoon is that the rules change on the outside; only old satellite technology to rely on out here.

A gleeful feeling grows inside me as we all step out into the heat. I breathe in the air: real and raw and heavy with desert dust. The others, even Yuke, are scowling under the bright glare. We get into formation, coarse sand and lichen crunching beneath our boots, and follow Charles towards a line of scrubby eucalypts on a nearby rise. I'm guessing he wants shade for whatever proceedings he has planned. As we draw nearer to the trees, I can smell their volatile oils drenching the sun-baked air. I feel like a cat let outdoors after months of confinement and have to restrain myself from running up the hill and burying my face in their leaves. I allow myself a long look at Anna at the front of the line. Her presence is regal, funereal. Sober enough, anyway, to bring my focus back to the task at hand.

They set the cage down at the top of the hill and the research team gathers around; some holding ECDs and some now holding small silver boxes I've not seen before. We close ranks behind them. At a signal from Charles, the guy with the long gloves steps forward, pops the lock and opens the cage door. Two of the researchers, a man and a woman, crouch down either side of the gloves-guy and help him drag the comatose dog out of the cage, kicking up fine dust as they dump him in the dirt. I glance at Anna. She's staring down at them, her eyes glazed over as though she has checked out.

I work out that gloves-guy is a dick pretty much immediately after that. He kicks the dog in the side. I see Anna flinch. Unnecessary. The big-shot's moment in the sun. Then he raises his hand in a dramatic signal to the other researchers, who come scurrying up to form a ring around the dingo.

"On my count!" he shouts, even though they're right next to him. They all raise their ECDs and their silver boxes. He shunts a needle into the dingo's thigh, hurries back a few paces and raises his own weapon.

"Five, four, three, two…"

The dingo opens its eyes and jumps to its feet. It bares its teeth, hunkers down into a crouch then leaps into the air.

"NOW!"

There is a ring of flashes from each of the boxes. In the white glare we can all see the dingo twisting violently in the air; stretching and breaking in all the wrong places until, with a last turn and a pain-wracked scream, a naked man falls to the ground with a thud.

Anna runs forward, elbowing her way through the wide-eyed onlookers, and collapses beside the man. She places her hands on either side of his face.

"Gardner." Her voice is a whisper, but it carries easily in the shocked silence.

He opens his eyes, a startling blue, more like a Huskie's than a dingo's, and reaches up to her, his hands smoothing her hair, her cheek. It's as though they're completely alone, such is the intensity of their connection. I watch their reunion as though I'm watching a movie, forgetting for a moment whose side I'm on and what I'm meant to be doing.

"Very touching, I'm sure." Charles steps forward and throws some clothes at Gardner. He grabs them with one hand, stands up and pulls them on.

"Where's my daughter?" Gardner addresses Charles with a voice gravelly from lack of use.

"Anna, tell him," says Charles with a jerk of his head. "All right, let's give them a few moments to say goodbye." He gestures to the retinue to follow him into the deep shade of a larger eucalypt, about fifty metres away. I follow, dragging my heels at the end of the line. Yuke gives me a perplexed look.

"Come on," he whispers, beckoning.

"You go ahead. I need to pee," I tell him.

His face relaxes, and he nods and hurries off. I slip behind the line of eucalypts, making my way back to where Anna and Gardner are standing, and crouch low amongst the shrubbery. I toy with finishing them both off straight away, but curiosity gets the better of me. I can see Anna's back, just metres from me; her long, strong legs, the flicker of her brown hands as they talk.

"They've tried it on me before. At least twice that I can remember. It only lasted a few minutes at first. The next time, a few hours." It's Gardner's voice, less rough now, reassuring.

"But this must be what they've been working on. What if they've perfected it, made it so it's permanent? You'll never last out there like this during the day on your own."

"I'm not going to stay out here. There's no way the deal stands, Anna."

"Maybe it's for the best."

"What do you mean?"

"Well, he's not going to just give up, is he? It might even mean a final crackdown on the Outdwellers. It'd put my mother and everyone in danger if I went back now."

"Do you *want* to stay with him?"

"No!"

There's silence.

"No," she says again. "I just want us all back together and I want to go home."

"Then we'll work out a way."

They hold each other in silence, pressing together.

A plume of dark heat sinks into my stomach and my heart hits against my ribcage as though it wants to get out. I ready my pistol with a quiet click, fighting the nausea. One silent shot to take them both out. And then I'll run, downslope and away. I swallow down the bile, try to ignore the roar of blood in my ears and the slick sweat on the metal in my hands as I steady the crosshairs over her heart.

27

FAULK

"What's up, princess?"

I whirl around. The two guards from the car are approaching me. I've seen looks on faces like that before. Looks that say they're the last thing you're gonna see. I edge my pistol down amongst the grass, trusting they haven't seen it, only my crouching position.

"Taking a dump?"

I stand up, one hand behind my back.

"Getting his rocks off watching the lovebirds, more like," says the other guard. They angle in at me from either side; two leering hyenas, the red haze of the hunt on their slack faces.

I decide in a split second and leap into the shrubs behind me. The guards press in after me. I scramble through until I've burst into the clearing. Anna pulls away from Gardner and whips around. Our eyes meet and her face goes pale.

I yell at her: "Get out of here!"

She startles like a roo, and with one glance in the direction of the hollering, jeering guards behind me, she grabs

Gardner's hand and pulls him after her, sprinting off across the rise beneath the cover of the trees, away from Charles and his wilting retinue. I whirl around to face the guards as they emerge from the bushes and have them down in two shots. Blood is already pooling from them where they lie in the dust, but I don't look too closely, just turn and sprint in the only direction open to me now, after Anna and Gardner.

~

ANNA

Gardner and I don't yet dare to emerge from our rocky hideout. We heard the last shouts and cries fade over two hours ago, but even as I know my father and his people are not equipped to remain outside the Dome for long, I find it hard to imagine them giving up before nightfall and wonder if the darkness truly will bring us safety.

I hunch inwards, Freya's face floating in the blackness behind my closed eyes.

"He *wouldn't* hurt her, would he?"

My voice is a whisper, but Gardner hears me and shakes his head.

"She's the only card in his hand right now. Your father is many things, but he's no fool."

My heart's thudding in my chest.

"What have we done to her?"

"Nothing yet."

"Do you think they're gone?"

"I don't know."

We lapse into silence, and he closes his eyes. He's sitting in a pool of light with his sleeves rolled up, the shafts of late afternoon sun slanting in through the hole in the cave roof miraculously holding no power over him.

"What does it feel like?"

He opens one eye.

"I mean—"

"To be human?"

"You've always been human. In the daylight, though…is it strange?"

He nods slowly. "Strange, yes."

I don't expect him to elaborate, but he opens both eyes and looks at me.

"And…weak."

I go and kneel in front of him and slide my hands along the insides of his arms until they're resting over his biceps.

"You feel strong to me."

His muscles push up beneath my palms as he draws me close.

"How strong?"

I lean in and press my lips to the hollow of his collarbone. His grip tightens and his breathing shallows.

"Very strong," I whisper, planting kisses up his neck, across his stubbled cheek and onto his mouth.

His lips part under me in a gasp, then he pulls me to him, crushing his mouth against mine, drinking me in. His hands find my skin and their heat fans through me as he draws back, his blue eyes dark.

"Is this…do you…?"

"Yes," I say, unhooking my shirt, removing my clothes, trying to answer his myriad unspoken questions with a look and that simple word.

He draws me close, but within moments he is grasping and biting and driving into me, hurting me with the ferocity of his touch. I find his face, place my hands against his cheeks to tell him, to slow him down. They're wet. When he meets my gaze, I see it all there for a flicker of a second; pain and betrayal, naked and unanswered. He swings off me and rolls onto his back.

I sit up beside him, wanting to hold him, needing to provide comfort.

Wordlessly, he reaches out and, more gently this time, pulls me to him. I sink down, bringing him deeply inside me, no longer able to read his expression in the shadow I'm casting upon his face.

We lie skin to skin as the golden light disappears. His breathing is even now, but my pulse is still racing. I close my eyes and will myself to drift to sleep. But a dark eagle rises to fill my vision, its wings outstretched against a pale sky, talons bearing down on me. I start and cry out. Gardner flinches but doesn't awaken.

I get up, suddenly cold, and try to find my clothes in the dark. Piece by piece, I retrieve them and pull them on. Then I stumble across the cave floor, climb up through the narrow entrance and out into the night.

The air is mild. A thin layer of cloud diffuses the bright bulb of the moon like a lampshade, providing enough light that I can see the boulders all around me, like shrouded giants hunched in sleep. The roof of our cave is a large, gently sloping wedge of rock. I walk to its edge, searching for any lights in the flats below us to the south. Nothing moves in the night-shadows.

To my right, the sky has its own glow. I pick my way carefully towards it, looking back now and then so as not to lose sight of the distinctive rock that marks our hideout. The moon is high in the sky and the stratus clouds in front of it are barely moving, so I have no fear that I'll lose my night lamp. Finally, after pushing through a small patch of shrubs and scaling a large, rippled rock, I reach the vantage point I'm after.

Below me, in an unbroken 180-degree panorama, I can see the last undulations of the landscape before it smooths into the basaltic flatlands that extend all the way to the Dome. From here, the Dome is breathtakingly beautiful: vast, curved and glowing.

Only now, far enough away from the heat of Gardner, do I allow myself to think about our escape. About the guard who had looked so like Faulk. If it really was him, why had he helped us? He had inflicted my bullet wound. I'd been so sure of that. Had I been wrong? I bring my hands to my forehead and stare across the plain, trying to make sense of it all. The white eye in the desert glares balefully back at me.

My mind is fuzzy with tiredness; nothing can make sense tonight. I turn to go. As I do, I hear a cracking sound, close to me, from a clump of bushes. My mouth turns dry with fear. I back up against the nearest rock and freeze, my ears straining into the night for another sound, for any further clue. But although I remain still for several minutes, I hear nothing else.

Eventually, I slide around the other face of the rock and head back down, moving as quickly as I can in the semi-darkness. I find my way back to our cave and hurry into it, jumping the last bit onto the floor. Gardner is still sleeping heavily. I lie down next to him, pull his discarded clothes over both of us and curl into his warmth, squeezing my eyes shut and listening into the silence until I fall asleep.

IN THE MORNING, the light through the entry point in our roof is blinding. I open my eyes and reach out for Gardner, but my hand meets empty space. I sit up with a start and look around the cave. Then I see him, sitting in a shaft of sunlight, watching me, his paws set neatly together, his tail curled around them.

"Oh." I can't keep the disappointment out of my voice.

Muscles above his eyes twitch and he raises his head to the exit above us. I get up, gather his clothes together and hoist the bundle onto my back. As we scramble to the surface, my stomach growls with hunger. I'm thirsty too, and thankful there's a stream nearby.

We make our way warily through the boulder field and, after detecting no sight or sound of pursuit, continue down to the banks of the creek. As we gradually release our caution and wade into the water to get our faces wet and drink our fill, I begin to wish we'd made some concrete plans together before he'd transformed. I suppose I thought he might never change back, and in some deep place in my heart, I know I'd hoped he might remain a man forever. I submerge my face in the freezing water. But then he would not be fully himself. His self-acceptance was one of the things I loved about him. How could I ask for that to be compromised? And yet. I'd had a taste of something different yesterday, some other possibility for us. And today that possibility sits gleaming and glinting like a river stone begging to be picked up and pocketed.

I retreat to the bank to dry, and I watch him chasing fish in the shallows. Eventually he catches one. The silver thing glints as it thrashes back and forth in his muzzle. He opens his mouth a fraction to readjust its weight, and the fish leaps back into the water. A plume of its blood is pulled into the current. It tries to wriggle itself into a deeper part of the channel, but Gardner's paws land on it again. He grasps it with his teeth and bashes it against the upper half of a submerged log. Even though I long to look away, I fix my gaze on it throughout its dying because it seems disrespectful somehow not to bear witness to its pain. Finally, its tail stops flapping and its mouth ceases to draw in desperate gulps of air.

We fill our stomachs with the raw fish and some young dandelion leaves I find in a moist soak by the stream. After we've eaten, we wash off in the water and lie out to dry in the sunshine. Then I follow Gardner back up through the boulders to the cave, realising as we clamber down into it, that he too must want to formulate a plan when we can speak. Too much depends on the next step we take. I reconcile myself to another night sleeping on cold, hard rock, another night without our daughter, and I send a silent plea to Sirena, hoping that the strength I glimpsed in her will mean Freya is in safe enough hands for now.

28

FAULK

I don't mean to follow their tracks, but they've taken the most efficient route along the crest of the rise and downwards where it drops towards to level ground. I run like never before, aware that it's only a matter of minutes before Charles works out that something's not right. I need only find somewhere to bunker down until they've caught Anna and dog-man. I needn't be missed or searched for, as long as Yuke holds his tongue. I realise I'm counting on his sense of being in my debt, but he also seemed a naïve stickler for the rules, so I don't kid myself that I'll be out of the firing range forever. Still, I'd rather be in my position than Anna's right now.

The rise ends in a tangle of bushes and some sedges at the base of the dune. I race through them, their spiky leaves catching at my legs. I can't see Anna in front of me and I wonder at that, as ahead of me is a vast expanse of exposed ground with nowhere to hide. I decide to make a hairpin turn around the other side of the dune so as to stick with the shrubby vegetation, hoping it'll afford me some cover. I pick up their tracks in a moist patch of sand. They've done the same. It's cooler on this southern face and soon I'm making my way through a copse of eucalypts. I stumble on, running as best I can through the clawing undergrowth.

A good ten minutes later, I hear the first faint shouts behind me from up the rise. I hurry on, scanning for a hollow in the landscape or a sturdy enough tree to climb. But there's nothing suitable and I'm forced to continue on.

Now I'm following a trickle of water that joins a larger creek coming in from the south. I step into the flow, grateful for the opportunity to leave no tracks, and follow its snaking trail around the base of the dune. Before long, I'm wading knee deep, thankful for the cooling water. I make it to the other side and emerge heavy and dripping. Then I run as best I can across the clearer ground beneath a canopy buzzing with the hum of bees and the squawking of lorikeets. Although the angled leaves allow some sunlight through to the ground, I find even this small shade a relief.

The stream, which is becoming wider and more defined, winds through a valley of boulders festooned with purple-flowered bushes growing from cracks between the rocks. A tall boulder by the edge of the water stands like a sentinel ahead of an advancing grey army tumbling down towards the river. I leave the bank and climb up amongst them. Rock-hopping and wedging myself through narrow fissures and across ever-deepening crevasses, I finally find a wind-sculpted hollow beneath an overhanging boulder, just large enough for me to back up into. I scramble into it and rest against the cool rock, my ears straining into the silence.

IT'S morning and I watch them by the river, pressing my scope up against my eyes. I'm surprised by their boldness. Gardner, a dingo again, can't sense me from my rocky perch downwind and shows no sign of alarm. And Anna. Anna. Stripped bare and splashing liquid-silver scoops of water onto her face. She's all that I remember. Full and brown, strong and smooth, her red hair loose; a water nymph now; no longer the wary fox. Gardner is watching her too, resting on his hindquarters, his face trained on her every move.

I watch her dive into the river. She's under for ages. Eventually I see her rise further along, water streaming down her body. This thwarts my attempts to think. I try to focus on something else. But all I land on is the memory of her when I first brought her into the city, the wetness I glimpsed blossoming at her breast before she crossed her arms to hide it. At first, this doesn't help at all. Until I remember the cause. Remember her daughter. The way the girl had looked at me when I gave her back the stone. The wary gratefulness in her face when I handed over my old book. This brings me around as though I've taken a dive into the cold water myself. Where's the girl now? With her grand-father, I guess. An unpleasant feeling starts in my gut. She was supposed to be next. Not just next, but the most impor-tant target, according to Goldengass. I can't find the anger in me now that made me promise to kill a child.

29

ANNA

"It's the only option Gardner."

The last of the light vanishes from the cave and he pulls on his clothes, all except his shirt, which he bunches into a makeshift pillow for us for the night.

"You're not going back there."

"I've worked it over and over in my mind. There's no other way. I need to be with Freya tomorrow. I can't let her go through the Change alone. You have to go home. Warn Mum and the rest of them. I'll get out when I can. It might take days, or weeks, but I'll come back."

He's silent, his fingers bridged and tense, massaging his forehead. Finally, he stands up.

"You're going to need Dr Kuanyin."

I nod. "I know. Sirena gave me an interfacer. I'll be able to get in touch with Lin as soon as I get back inside."

"I still don't like it."

"Neither do I, but can you see any other way?"

Gardner scrutinises my face and sees the set lines there.

"Be careful."

"If I go before dawn, then at least I'll have cover for a while."

"I'll see you down to the other side."

"No. I can manage. You need to start heading home. The sooner Mum knows the better."

"Then let's get some rest."

He pulls me down to lie beside him and holds me to his chest. I close my eyes and breathe him in. We sleep like that until the first kookaburras call.

I sit up in the dark, gently prizing his arm off me. He breathes sharply and rolls onto his back. I stroke my thumb against his temple as I would with Freya to ease her back to sleep.

"Goodbye, my love."

I press my lips lightly to his. His eyes flash open, and he grasps my waist, pulling me against him in a deep kiss that sends sparks of heat all through me. His palms press and circle like fire and I arch into him. I want to stay here always like this with his body against mine, his hands dancing skilfully across my skin. So as not to think. So as not to fear.

The kookaburras call again, and he springs to his feet. I glance up at the faintly glowing crack of sky above us. Dawn is coming.

"Look after yourself. Tell Freya I love her. I *will* see you soon," he says with a last kiss.

I nod, unable to speak for fear of tears spilling out and making me forget to be brave.

I climb up and out onto the ledge. The sky is pinker and lighter than I'd hoped. I peer down into the cave to see Gardner looking up at me, his blue eyes bright.

Light hits my face—the sun bursting above the horizon.

"Goodbye!" I call into the gloom.

I hear nothing at first, but then my words are answered

by a mournful howl.

I make my way up to the spot I'd explored the night before last, hoping that from here I'll be able to see the easiest way down the other side. In the daylight, the boulders loom larger and the depths seem more dizzying. The early morning breeze shifts into a stronger wind and I have to keep a tight hold of the crevices with my fingers and flatten myself against the rocks in order to clamber over the last boulder before the top. The wind has turned to a gale by the time I reach the lookout point. I slide down against an upright tor to shield myself from the blast and try to peer out over the plain. The way seems fairly sheer down the south-west side, so I chance the boulders on the south-eastern face, even though it looks the more circuitous route.

The wind threatens to prise me off the rocks with each gust. I stick to the sheltered sides of boulders and scale the inside edges of ravines, just to keep out of the gale. Eventually, with my palms and fingertips red raw and my feet aching, I worm inside a wind-sculpted hollow to rest for a bit. My stomach growls with hunger and my throat feels parched.

After a while, the wind eases. The first fat drops of rain turn quickly into a deluge and I hunch into my shelter, my heart sinking as I watch the boulders become slick with the downpour. Now they'll be too slippery; it'd be foolish to risk descending any further until the rain has stopped and the granite has had time to dry. I scuff at the cave floor and roar in frustration.

My roar turns to a cry of surprise as, with a wet scuffle, a pair of booted feet appear at the entrance to my shelter. I back up mutely against the wall as someone squeezes their way in. As the figure straightens, shaking off sprays of water from tangled, dark hair, I find myself face-to-face with Faulk

Parker. My gut churns with fear and relief in equal measure; the relief, with no basis, as Shama's warning bellows in my ears: 'Anna, beware!'. I look for a sign of the same fight playing out across his features, but I cannot see it. He draws his weapon.

The rain drums hard against the rocks. I close my eyes, bracing for pain, hoping he'll be quick. Freya is all I can see as I watch the rest of her life; a life without me in it, spool out on the black screen of my mind.

He says something, but I can't hear the words for the ringing in my ears.

"Anna."

I open my eyes.

"I'm going to lower my weapon. If you so much as twitch a muscle, I'll shoot you through without hesitation."

I remain perfectly still as he lowers the gun.

"There," he says and takes a heavy step forward.

A new stab of fear turns at the base of my spine. I press my back against the cold cave wall as though it might allow me to disappear into it.

He lunges, seizing me by the upper arm and ripping me away from the rock. I try to wrench out of his grasp, but he snatches hold with his other hand. I kick at him, but he grabs me behind my raised knee and pulls me so close that I can feel his hot breath on my face. Feigning a slackening of my body, I try a sudden flinch out of his hold, but he is quicker and tightens his grip. I can't move. Time seems to expand so that I notice a myriad of small details: the transition from stubble to smooth skin illuminated by a square of light on his cheek, the snarled line of his lips, the wet smell of his clothes. And in that long, clear moment gifted to me, I make one decision: that whatever happens now, I will not look away. I will be my own witness.

I stare into his shadowed face, and it is a stare that is hard and bold and fierce as a bird of prey. I don't know if this alters the black energy within him or if something else gives him pause, but I see a deep furrow form between his eyes.

His grip tightens and then releases, throwing me backwards and off balance, knocking my breath out of me as I slam against the wall of the cave. I stagger upright and try to find some strength in my limbs so that this time I can fight him.

But there is no release for the coiled-up springs of my muscles because he is not coming towards me. He has turned his back on me. For several seconds, I stare at his dark silhouette, waves of nausea washing through my body.

Then I see him collapse into a crouch, and he begins shuddering as though he's a puppet on a violently shaken string. It's only when I hear a low, strangled sound that I understand he is crying.

I tread quickly and quietly towards the cave entrance, intent on running, on chancing the climb down the slippery boulders to flee for my life. But as I'm about to step out into that oval of light, I find myself stopping and turning around.

With my mind screaming at me to leave, I edge towards him, reach out to touch the wet fabric of his coat with my fingertips, and then with my whole hand. I can feel his back heaving up and down beneath my palm. Then he begins rocking, backwards and forwards. Slowly, I move around to kneel in front of him. He has his hands up, covering his face like a child. He doesn't even flinch as I reach out and take hold of one of his wrists. There is no resistance as I pull him close and hold him until tears and animal howls start to pour out of him in great, shuddering gasps.

It seems an age before he quietens. The rainstorm eases outside and sunlight is visible at the entrance. I look down at his face, reminded of when I found him sleeping at the wetlands.

His eyes flash open as if he's been startled awake, and he scrambles to sit.

"Anna—"

"Shhh. It's all right."

"No. Nothing's all right."

He looks down at the weapon lying discarded beside us. A twinge of fear rises in me again. But he kicks at the gun and it goes skidding across the floor of the cave until it hits the wall.

"What would Mia think of me now? I've done it all wrong."

I want to scream at him: "*Yes, you have!*". But I say nothing.

"She was so brave. So powerful." His voice is a thin whisper, but I can feel only the merest of sluice gates holding back the howling torrent of a moment ago. "I remember. She became this...this wild force. This woman I never knew was in her. And she did it. She did it!" His words speed up with their free fall from within him. "He was so little. So much smaller than I ever thought a newborn would be—all dark and wrinkled. He had this waxy gunk on him. I didn't know they came out like that. It was probably ugly. But I loved it, loved him. As soon as I saw him, I knew I'd give up my life for him. But I didn't. I didn't."

"You didn't have a chance to."

"If I hadn't gone home. Hadn't left them alone."

I say nothing, allowing the cave and the silence to hear him.

"We had this list of names. She had some crazy ones in there. But she was like that. A crazy girl. So funny. Hopeful and full of life. She was so much stronger than me."

He is looking up and to his left. To his ghosts.

"But we didn't get a chance to name him."

"She did." The words slide out before I can stop them.

"What?"

"She gave him a name." I speak quickly and quietly, wishing I hadn't spoken at all.

"What do you mean?"

"She called him 'Orion'."

Faulk breathes in sharply and gets to his feet, shaking me off.

"But that was on our list! How did you know??"

I regret telling him, regret bringing the focus of attention back to myself when my position is so precarious.

I shake my head. "I'm sorry."

Suspicion clouds his eyes. Then he stands up and starts pacing around me.

"What else do you know Ms Drake? Is Goldengass right? That you're a sorcerer and a terrorist; that you want to destroy the Dome?"

"I don't want to destroy anything. I just want to find Freya and go home."

He stops in front of me and crosses his arms.

"But what are you not telling me?"

I look up at him.

"Freya..."

"Freya what? What are you all up to with her?"

"Gardner—" I say his name quietly, as though to invoke his presence here will do further damage to this already damaged man. "Her father's first transformation occurred on his fifth birthday. Freya turns five tomorrow. Tomorrow, my daughter is going to change into an animal and I'm scared that I won't be there when it happens. The only reason we came to the city was so my little girl didn't have to go through that alone, to stop it if we could. Because it was frightening and painful for her father when it first started happening. There's an expert in the city who knows how to help; who can provide pain relief, tutelage—things Gardner always wished he'd had. That's all."

Faulk starts to pace again.

"Then Goldengass was right about the sorcery in your family. So why should I believe you're not planning an act of terrorism?"

I stand up so that I'm level with him.

"Because I am not a terrorist."

His laugh is harsh, almost hysterical. I scramble for something else, something that will convince him.

"And because now I know that it's my own father who is at the heart of this…this campaign of misinformation."

He stops pacing and looks me square in the face.

"But it's a kill order. For you, your daughter, Gardner. Why would your father want you all dead?"

I shake my head, a sudden heaviness settling in my bones.

"I don't know. I don't think he does. Gardner maybe. But I can't believe me or Freya."

"I wouldn't put it past Goldengass to run with the intel his own way. Unless…" He cocks his head to one side as though appraising the issue from another angle. Then he laughs again; a hollow, humourless sound that echoes around the cave.

"Unless?"

"Unless they expected me to fail. Maybe your father doesn't want you dead, only scared."

I rub wearily at my forehead. "That's possible, especially given my last conversation with him."

We both stare out towards the light. The only sound is the occasional drip of water from the overhang onto the rocks below.

"So...you're not going to stop me?"

"I'm not at all sure I would have taken a shot in this cave, anyway."

I shiver as I recall the strange pushing sensation behind my shoulder before I'd passed out in my father's doorway. The sensation I now realise was the bullet entering my flesh.

"What *will* you do then?"

"Well, I've ditched my chip. I could be a free man somewhere far away from the Dome. Or...I could come and help you find your daughter."

I stare at him.

"I have a lot to make up for, Anna. This'd be a start. But... only if you want me to. I mean...if you feel you can trust me."

I say nothing.

"Could you...do you...trust me?"

"No."

There's a hot buzzing starting up through my fingers. I open and close my hands to get the feeling away. He doesn't move, as though his ears are straining into the moment before the judge hands down the verdict. As though what I say now will either heal him or break him forever. But there is nothing I can say. All I can feel now is the pins and needles moving up into my arms, the bruises beginning on my back where he pushed me against the rock, and my dry throat.

"Have you got water in that pack of yours?"

He takes out the water bottle and passes it to me. I take a cold, clear gulp and hand it back to him.

He looks down at the bottle. "I'm so deeply sorry, Anna. For hurting you. Then and now."

I look at him, allowing the words in. Then I nod slowly. "Well, I used you to try to get what I needed. I'm sorry for that."

He shakes his head. "You didn't have much choice."

I scuff at the tiny grains of quartz and flecks of mica glinting up at me from the cave floor. "We all have choices."

"Whatever you...or we...did, back in the Dome," he continues, "it made me...well...I can feel things again. It hurts like hell. But it's better than before."

I meet his eyes, bright again with water, and begin to shiver, my body suddenly so weak I have to sit back down.

"Here." He takes off his coat and drapes it around me. "It's the adrenaline. You're in shock."

He pulls a container from his backpack, takes a flat biscuit out of it, and hands it to me.

"Go on; the sugar will help."

After I've eaten and had a little more water, I find I have more strength in my limbs. I try standing up. The world is not quite steady, but a few deliberate steps towards the entrance seem to help. I take off his coat and hand it back to him.

"It looks dry enough outside. Shall we go?"

He nods, his eyes clear with relief, and we both re-enter the daylight, blinking against the glare.

The climb down is easier once we settle into a rhythm. His longer stride length comes in handy when we're crossing the larger crevasses and my nimbler climbing enables me to scale large boulders now and then to scout the way forward through the maze of slippery rocks and ravines. Bit by bit, moment by moment, we inch towards a kind of trust in each other.

When we finally jump off the last rocky shelf he gives me a broad smile that brings an unfamiliar lightness and youth to his features.

We spend the next half an hour looking for a water source at the base of the hill. Eventually, Faulk finds some at a mossy ledge a little further east; no doubt a meagre trickle on any other day, but today, bolstered by the downpour, it is fresh and strong. We drink as much as we can and refill his water bottle. I search around for anything edible but can find nothing other than a few prickly currant bush berries which aren't quite ripe. I pick them anyway; they are tart and astringent on my tongue. I hand Faulk the last couple and he throws them into his mouth and then pulls a face.

"You'd have to be really hungry to eat these."

"We *are* really hungry."

"Hungrier then." He strides away from the rocks and water and into the New Desert sand. "Come on, let's go find your girl."

FAULK

The new lightness in my body seems to permeate everything: the sunshine glinting off the trickling water; the green velvet of the moss carpeting the rock; the grey sand, grading to orange as we range further from the boulders; the deep fire-red of her hair. It takes me a while to realise that this unfamiliar state of being is joy; something I haven't felt for a god-awful amount of time. And if I'd known that Mia and our son would feel closer to me than ever in this state, I would have chosen, if I could not find joy, then something at least akin to it, a long a time ago.

I am drunk on our journey. High on her forgiveness, her spirit, her compassion, her fierce will. Hers is a quest I can truly commit to. And I know now I will follow her wherever she needs me to go.

30

GARDNER

*I*t is the scent I catch on the blasting wind that
decides me. Having travelled, leaping rock to
rock, back the way we'd come, I am drinking some river-
water and contemplating catching myself another fish when
a breeze whistling up through a crevasse stops me mid-
drink. My fur raised and nose to the wind, I take longer
sniffs, bringing the traces to me until a picture forms in my
mind. It is the man, Faulk, and I can smell his desire in the
small molecules that float to meet my canine senses.

It had felt so very wrong to be leaving her, anyway. The
further north I'd moved, the more uncomfortable I'd
become. This clear signal, calling me from kilometres away,
is more than enough to make me turn around and bolt off in
a race to retrace my steps, my only hope now that I might
reach Anna in time.

The downpour begins minutes before I reach our original
hideout. I clamber past it, but my paws, even with their claws
and rough pads, slip on the slick rocks. There's no chance I'll
return to our cave, not with so urgent a task ahead, but it is a

dire and risky climb I make to the top of the outcrop. I pause at a spot that looks out over the plain all the way to the Dome, trying to work out the route Anna would have taken. The rain has washed away a lot of her scent, but it seems clear she would have chosen the less sheer route to the south-east.

I try and shake off some of the driving rain and suddenly find myself assaulted by the scent of the man again, so near that I'm surprised it has taken me this long to sense it.

Behind the lookout spot is a patch of shrubs. I nose my way in. There is a wind-sculpted shelter, hidden from view behind the wall of shrubs. I push into it. His traces are all around here, his scent lingering on the rock, pungent in the moist air, suggesting he was here for a while: a day and a night at least, possibly more. So close to us. Clearly hunting us—or at least, Anna—as he must have made a great attempt to remain downwind of me at all times. How foolish I was, so caught up in my own challenges that this possibility never occurred to me.

The rainstorm worsens, as though a giant in the sky has pulled the plug from a bathtub, unleashing water on the earth in a torrent. I must wait it out or be washed down the mountain in a flood. I pace the shelter, damning the downpour, my howls lost in the hashing of the waterfall now flowing over the jutting rock shelter. My blood fizzes and churns with impatience and dread for Anna and anger at my stupidity.

Finally, I settle on the cold rock and bury my nose beneath my tail, closing my eyes in an attempt to stop the images flickering across the screen of my mind. It does no good. I can find no peace when all I can see is her face and all I can smell is his blood.

31

ANNA

*I*t's as though it never rained. The desert sand is almost dry and we're trudging beneath the cloudless sky with the sun in our eyes. I find myself almost enjoying Faulk's company. In his new, released state, I catch glimpses of the man Mia must once have known. He picks pigface leaves for us to eat as we walk—salty but moist and crunchy—and tells me how he and his brother, Kes, had once collected the bright pink flowers from the dunes on the beach to take home for their mother. How their mother had thrown them out, telling them that foraged plants were beneath them now that they lived in the city, and how Kes had retrieved them and given them to his girlfriend instead. The gentle crease lines around his eyes when he talks about his brother are unfamiliar to me. I figure he must have smiled a lot once. But then I don't think too much more on it because the bruises where he grasped my arms back at the cave are beginning to throb.

We decide to skirt around the Night Market, as many of the stallholders would already be setting up for the evening.

Thankfully, my interfacer works now that we're near the Dome, so finally, I can call Lin.

We find a spot to the west of the campsite, in the long shade of a clump of eucalypts humming with insects. We guzzle the last of our water and then Faulk wanders off a little way and I call Dr Kuanyin. Her face appears, shimmering at first and then settling.

"Anna! I'm relieved to see you."

"Lin. Can you come and pick us up? We're at the North Gate, just west of the Night Market campsite. We don't dare come any closer."

"Of course. Give me half an hour."

Her image flickers and dissipates.

I release a long breath and look across at Faulk, who is adjusting his belt, his face a question.

"She's coming."

"Here?"

"Yes."

He sits down in the dust. "Then I guess we wait."

I nod and find a spot opposite him. "I guess we wait."

GARDNER

In the absence of their trails, obliterated by the rain, I navigate my own way through the boulder-field, trusting I'd pick up their scent if they were still up here; hoping she made it all the way down without interference.

I discover their tracks at the base of the climb. They puzzle me at first. There's no sign of a struggle, just crisscrossing, weaving trails along the base of the mountain. They lead me, finally, to a rivulet running off a rock ledge at which

I drink my fill. From here, their tracks strike out into the desert and I can see that he is ahead of her, probably pulling her along behind him. This is enough for me. With a growl, I leap off after them across the sand.

ANNA

As we wait for Lin, Faulk draws with a small stick in the sand. I watch his dusty, brown hands, his fingers moving with a precision that's almost graceful.

I get up and pace. The insects have stopped their droning in the flowering eucalypt above our heads and a flock of rainbow lorikeets have begun a raucous pre-roost chorus. I watch them flapping and preening, their colours saturated in the golden light.

A movement in the corner of my vision makes me turn from the parrots to the direction from which we have come. A speck is growing on the horizon—no, coming nearer. For a confused moment, I think it's Gardner, even though it can't be. I turn to Faulk, who's on his feet, staring out in the same direction.

Then, without warning, a heart-stopping boom blasts through the earth, confounding our senses. The lorikeets take to the air, ripping apart the sky with their rasping squawks. Faulk and I pivot to the source of the sound. The North Gate is on fire; huge orange plumes shafting upwards, licking the edges of the Dome like a demonic mouth. As we watch, a sudden wash of water falls down on the flames from the Dome itself, and the slices and spangles of fire and water, sunlight and shattered pieces of rainbow dazzle my eyes. I drop to the ground and press my chest to my knees. Faulk throws himself over me, shielding me with his body. I look out through the cracks between my fingers; a golden sphere is expanding rapidly outwards from the site of the explosion towards us. I brace and squeeze my eyes shut. Faulk's fingers tighten against me.

But all I feel as it passes through us is a shimmer of heat, and then we're in a giant bubble of some kind, and we're breathing what feels like the cool, moist air of a forest. I open my eyes. There is no forest. All is eerily silent.

Our gaze is drawn to the bright, white-golden centre of the sphere where a figure stands like a star, its arms and legs outstretched. Faulk and I get to our feet. Although I'm not moving, I feel as though I'm being drawn in towards the figure. At first I think it's Shama, her face is so radiant; her hair a wild, wind-whipped tangle around her. But it's not Shama. It is Freya. And her expression is one I've never seen before on my little girl: peaceful but alert, her eyes seeming to see with such clarity, her mouth lifted in an ecstatic smile. Then she sees me, and sighs, and the sound of it is as loud as a wave crashing against a shore.

"Mama!" Her voice rings through the sphere like the bright peal of a great bell. "Look at me!"

"Yes! Look at you my love. Look at you!"

And then Freya screams: "No!" and the sound almost blows out my ear-drums.

The golden bubble bursts. I see her, not thirty metres from me, and there are two others with her. Charles has Freya by the arm and Sirena seems to be trying to keep hold of her in a losing tug of war.

I break into a run, Faulk close at my heels. I've almost reached them when something dark flutters out of the sky and lands heavily on my shoulder with a loud flap in my ear and a digging of claws into my flesh. I suck in a surprised breath before I realise that it's Zotzi. I scan ahead for Lin but cannot see her. Then I realise there's someone lying on the ground between Freya and my father.

"Oh no!"

I run, and Zotzi flies ahead and lands next to Lin. She is still, her eyes closed and her arms flung out wide. His keening screeches tear at the air.

"Charles, what have you done?!"

I race towards him.

"Let go of my daughter!"

As I pull up in front of him, my father's face is mad with a kind of anger I only remember from my youth, from the days before we left him.

"Your daughter," he spits, "is a sorcerer! And you are no better. You brought this upon yourself. Upon us all!"

I blanch. I've never heard his fury fired so directly at me before.

Faulk steps out from beside me, his weapon drawn and directed at my father.

"Let her go." His voice is quiet, his gaze not wholly on Charles but flickering constantly to Zotzi, perched beside Lin's still form.

"You!" Charles sneers at Faulk. "A useless assassin turn-coat. Do you really think she'll warm to you if you shoot her father?"

Charles yanks Freya to him and Sirena, startled, loses her grip on her.

"Come now, Faulk, we don't suffer witches today any more than we ever did. Look behind me—look at the devastation this whelp has caused. Our work in ashes. You remember what it was like. When you lost your child, your family, to people like this!"

"No," says Faulk, "No." His voice and his gaze are steady

215

as he moves forward. "I lost them to people like you: bigots and ideologues; people who put the accrual of wealth and power ahead of anything, even their own flesh and blood."

Faulk doesn't stop until he's right up in Charles' face. Then he wrests Freya from his grip and turns with her to me. I meet his gaze, and I know he can feel my gratitude flowing into him. It lights him up and his eyes smile with it.

A deep growl sounds from behind me. Something streaks past in a sandy blur. Gardner. This time I'm sure of it. He reaches Faulk before I do, and the next sound I hear is a low cry.

I run forward, but Gardner has disappeared after Charles and I can't see Freya or Sirena anywhere.

And then all I can see is Faulk. Faulk, like a closing paper fan, falling to his knees; three long, red claw lines blossoming down his chest and across his stomach.

The instant I reach him, he collapses against me, his torso heavy on my awkwardly folded legs. Sticks and pebbles push up beneath me, but I daren't move for fear of breaking him further. He looks up as though from the bottom of a lake, his breathing a harsh staccato.

"Hold on, just...you need to hold on," I tell him.

He shakes his head; a small, weak gesture. "I knew it. Knew she'd come for me eventually."

"No."

With difficulty, he lifts his hand to rest over mine.

"I've never missed a target, but I'm glad I missed you. You brought me back to life."

He coughs and bright blood spatters his lips.

"Just don't try to talk."

"I need to know...if it's true." His voice is a ragged whisper.

"If what's true?"

"Orion?"

"Yes," I say, my eyes stinging.

"Good. That's good. That was the only one we both liked...it sounded like the name of a good person. I wanted him to be a good person."

Then his body spasms and his eyes widen.

"Mia—"

"Faulk!"

His chest heaves to a stop. His hand slides down by his side and he's suddenly heavy against me. I shake him, but it does no good. I hold him because I won't let him down into the dirt.

Then Sirena is there, pulling me from under Faulk's body, lifting me to my feet. Desert dust billows where he falls. He is in the dust. I can't tear my eyes from him. Sirena snatches hold of me. Places her hands either side of my face. Demands that I see her.

"Come on!"

I snap to her face, her white hair loose from its braiding, her blue eyes wide with terror. It's only then that I notice someone else behind her, bent over with their hands on their knees as though catching their breath. Zotzi flutters to the ground between us and the figure straightens.

"Lin!" I rush towards her, a relieved sob convulsing my chest. "I thought you were dead!"

I embrace her. Too tightly. She winces.

"Just bruised. It'll take more than a push to finish me off."

"We have to go!" urges Sirena, "I can't see Charles or Freya anymore!"

I nod. "Which way did they go?"

"Follow me."

Sirena heads off at a sprint towards the North Gate and we run after her, Zotzi flying at Lin's side. As we run, the sun sinks on the horizon so that soon we can hardly see where we're placing our feet and Zotzi is no longer flying.

"Go ahead, we'll catch up!" calls Lin, as she and Zotzi pull up behind us.

Eventually, the only light is from the smouldering embers of the North Gate. We keep running until my heart is bursting with pain and my legs are like wood. And then we are at the gate and I can see them, framed in the ruined arch as though they're performers in a shadow play. Gardner is growling, pacing around Charles, who has Freya in an iron hold.

As I watch, Gardner leaps into the air and his silhouette twists in an arc, his limbs shrinking and widening, head shortening, hands and feet lengthening until, at last, he lands in a crouch in front of Charles. He straightens, his eyes fixed on my father, the glowing coals lending his naked skin a gold sheen.

"Come on." Gardner grinds out. "Just you and me. Man to man."

Charles laughs. "That is not my style, brute. And you are no man."

I see a flash in the firelight and realise that Charles has a knife to Freya's throat. I feel as though I've been punched in the stomach.

"Ah, I see my daughter has decided to join our merry throng."

"What do you want from us?!" I shout.

"I thought we'd discussed this already."

I edge closer. Sirena stays back.

"So tell me again, where they all can hear!"

"I want you to forget this beast of yours and come with me into the city. I will not harm Freya if you agree to stay and forget your childish dalliances with this dropout class of futureless people. Freya will be taught ways to control herself and you will put your own skills to good use within the community that made you who you are and to whom you owe your respect and allegiance: good people working for the future of humanity. I will not see you waste your life and potential with ruffians who seek to destroy everything we have sought to build."

"And if I don't come with you?"

He digs the knife against her throat.

"All right, stop!"

I move so that I'm right in front of them, level with Gardner.

"First, I need to talk to Freya."

Charles' gaze on me is closed and cold. He does not move or release the knife from her skin. "Go on then."

I meet my daughter's terrified eyes.

"What did Lin say to you, love?

"No witch talk!" Charles' face whitens in fury.

"She gave me something to drink, that's all—"

"I said, no witch talk!"

Freya screams as Charles yanks her head back by the hair, pushing again with the knife.

"Freya!"

"Enough!" Charles' voice rings in my ears.

"Let her go and I will come with you. Freya will stay with her father."

Charles narrows his eyes, his furious gaze flitting between me and Gardner.

"It will be so much easier for you that way," I press.

"And you trust this brute with your child?"

"She is his child also."

To my surprise, he laughs.

"Foolish girl. You've always trusted too easily."

He turns to Gardner.

"Tell her."

I catch Gardner's startled look in the firelight.

"Tell her what?" he growls.

"Tell her what you told me, when your *daughter* was a mere babe in the womb."

I turn to Gardner. He says nothing, but neither does he meet my eye. Charles continues.

"He told me, dear Anna, what he was. And furthermore, that he was afraid his child would turn out to be a monster like himself, that she would kill her own mother as she birthed herself into the world. He asked me if there was anything I could do. Whether I knew anyone, with my substantial wealth and connections, who knew how to reverse such a curse or who could rid you of the child in a proper setting, in a hospital, with proper doctors."

I gasp. Gardner finally looks at me, his expression imploring.

"That was before I knew, before I understood!"

Charles sniffs, his face pure disdain.

"That's where you were when Freya was born!" I stare at him, horrified. "You were in the city?"

"And that's how he found me," comes a firm voice from behind me.

"Lin!"

"Yes, Anna. Gardner came to me then. I taught him all I could. He came to understand that he had a gift, not a curse. And I believe I put his mind at ease that you would be well and that his daughter, far from being a monster, would be his treasured child."

"And she is—you are, Freya. I knew very little about myself, about love at all, until you were born," says Gardner.

Freya's wide eyes stare at her father in the orange glow.

"I love you too Daddy."

"Enough!" shouts Charles. "Come on Anna. I weary of this performance. Come with me now and your dog shall have his child."

I take a step towards him, but Lin grasps my arm and hisses quickly into my ear.

"She needs no amplifier from me now."

I nod minutely and walk up to my father and Freya.

"I want to hold my daughter one last time before I have to leave her forever."

"No," says Charles.

I stare into his eyes, dark as stones, glittering in the firelight.

"Please grandfather," says Freya. "I will miss her so much. Please. Just one hug."

Before he has a chance to say no again, I reach out and Freya grasps my hand. Charles releases her into my arms and turns out to face Gardner, his knife raised in front of him.

As I bring Freya into my embrace, it is as though we are a lock and a key; there is only the familiar warmth and the perfect scent of her, my daughter, in my arms again. I bury my face in her hair and whisper into her ear.

"My darling, you are ready to do this by yourself. You don't need Lin's drink. Try again."

"That's enough." Charles' command cuts between us and he yanks Freya from me.

This time, the explosion is not as loud. It is a deep bass, like water being sucked up through a rocky blowhole. But the fire crackling around my daughter is real, and a fierce wave of heat blasts us before it dissipates into a glowing, golden sphere. Charles and I are both thrown to the ground by the force it. As we scramble to standing, Freya pulls the sphere back, breathing heavily with the effort. For a disoriented moment, my father and I look at each other. He no longer has the knife in his hand. Before I can look for where it landed, or work out what to do, Gardner runs between us and plants such a blow to Charles' head that it knocks him to the ground. He lies face-down in the sand, but after a moment I can see the shallow rise and fall of his chest. Gardner stands over him.

"Go. Take Freya and go!"

By the dying embers, I can see that Gardner has the wolf in his eyes.

"Gardner, that's enough."

He stares at me. "He tried to kill our daughter."

"He's still my father."

"All hell will rain on us, on your mother, on all the Outdwellers, if he's allowed to go back in there and gather his resources!" He jabs towards the Dome with his thumb.

"That might be so. But you've done enough killing."

A frown flickers between Gardner's brows.

"And this time you won't be able to justify it as the actions of a dog. I don't want that for you. I don't want that for Freya."

Freya grasps my hand, and I draw her in front of me and wrap my arms around her.

"Anna is right, Gardner," says Lin, who has hobbled up behind us.

"Then what do you suggest we do?" Gardner's voice is edged with frustration and, I realise now, a deep weariness.

"I can give him Oblivion."

"You have some?"

Lin nods. "Just a little."

"What will it do to him?"

"Two drops erases memories from the last year of your life."

"Can you give him more?" I ask.

Lin shakes her head. "No, that's all I have with me. It's merely my travelling set."

"So, he will still know about Freya and Gardner."

"He will."

I take in a long breath and exhale with force.

"Well, it's better than nothing. Thank you."

Lin reaches into a small pouch at her belt and draws out a tiny tincture bottle with a blue label. We roll Charles over and sit him up. I prise open his jaw and Lin places two drops on his tongue.

Sirena helps us move Charles to the ruins of his car and we arrange him inside it. We can already hear the sound of sirens from behind the blocked wreckage of the North Gate.

"Sirena," I say, "why did Charles come out here in the first place? How did he know we were here?"

Sirena bites her lip. "That interfacer I sewed into your clothes. It was a tracker as well. I'm sorry."

"Oh."

"I didn't know who to trust."

I nod. "I understand."

"I'll wait here with him," she says.

"Are you sure you don't want to come with us?" I ask.

Sirena shakes her head, smiling. "My life is in there. And it's a comfortable one. As long as you're sure Charles will have no memory of recent events, I don't see why I can't remain in his employ."

"You *are* sure, right Lin?" says Gardner.

"Perfectly," she says, "and now, I'm afraid we have to get going before the authorities get here; I'm sure none of us wish to be queried."

"You're coming with us?" Freya's face brightens.

"Of course. This is only the beginning of your learning, my dear. Zotzi and I have much to share with you."

WE FIND Faulk lying where he fell. Gardner keeps his distance, but I kneel next to him and Freya comes to sit beside me. To my surprise, she withdraws a round stone from her pocket and places it gently into the palm of his hand. Then she creates a sphere of perfect silence around us. It seems to come a little more easily for her this time—there is a pulse of heat, but no explosion, and it has a bright blue daytime sky.

The light of her golden sphere gives Faulk's drained face a glow again, as though he were only asleep. As we sit by him, a plaintive, echoing cry pierces the silence. A shadow falls on us and I look up to see a wedge-tailed eagle circling, soaring closer and closer out of Freya's enchanted sky with a single flap of its long-feathered wings. When it gets so close that I think it must land, it brushes the dark tip of one wing against Faulk's cheek and then rises again as though on a spiralling updraft. I follow it until it is high against the blue. Blinking in the glare, I lift a hand to shade my eyes, and when I look again, there are two eagles, circling each other, up and away.

32

ANNA

The relief that we're back together is enough to sustain us through the hours of walking until we make it to Meiying and Renshu's house. But as I knock on the door, hoping we're not disturbing them from their sleep, I can almost taste the heavy weight of everything left unsaid between Gardner and me.

We stand on their doorstep, apologising for the late hour, but Freya runs into Meiying's arms.

"No, not too late," Meiying says, holding Freya to her and shepherding her inside. "Come in, come in."

Renshu is already adding more chairs to the table strewn with bowls containing the remnants of their evening meal. He smiles and nods at Lin, and at Zotzi hovering by the door.

"Welcome, sit down, eat. I will make more."

He disappears into the kitchen and we all sit up at the table with Meiying. Soon we can smell delicious wafts of sizzling chilli and garlic.

"Your car—" begins Gardner.

Meiying waves his words away. "We can order another

for free from the Long Life League, no problem. We're just relieved you're safe."

As dishes of hot food are piled in front of us, I can think of very little but the taste and smell of it, the way it feels to fill my belly again. Gardner and Freya too are gulping down huge mouthfuls. Next to me, Lin eats with a precise delicacy and Zotzi picks at his plate, meeting nobody's gaze and hunching down into his seat.

Gradually, the food works its magic and we begin to talk.

"Zotzi," I say, as an impulse takes me. He looks startled to be addressed. "We are very much looking forward to you returning home with us. I hope you'll stay for a while. I know you and Gardner will have much to discuss, and Freya will be so happy to have someone her own age to spend time with."

His face breaks into a smile, and he looks at Lin.

"Do you like the sound of that, Zotzi?" she asks.

"Yes," he says, giving Freya a shy nod.

Freya grins back at him and picks up her spoon.

"Can you do this?" She tries to balance it on her nose. "I'm a koala.'

The spoon falls to the table with a clatter and Zotzi giggles.

"Did you know Mummy saw one once? When she was little."

"Oh!" says Zotzi, his bright eyes wide.

As Meiying folds her cloth napkin into the shape of a lotus for Freya and Zotzi's benefit, I turn quietly to Lin.

"Lin," my low whisper catches her attention. "Will Freya not turn into an animal at all then?"

"She will not. It seems, after all, that she is not a Spiritwalker like her father, but a Spiritweaver, like her mother."

"A Spirit...weaver?"

"Yes, as I told you, you have a powerful gift. How do you think you were able to have those visions?"

"You gave me drugs!"

"That was only an amplifier. The same as I gave your daughter."

"So…she inherited all that from me?"

Lin looks sidelong at me in the manner of a teacher waiting for a pupil to catch up. "Does what she can do not feel familiar to you?"

For a moment, the talk at the table seems to fade and I can feel the expansion of a memory within me: Shama's shining face beneath the glow of the sphere in that last, small pocket of forest. The trust and sadness in her eyes. The enormity of what she'd bequeathed to me in that small hour, when I did not know whether or not I dreamed, hits me now under Lin's scrutinising gaze.

"It was like the time Shama showed me the Heart of the World."

Lins nods slowly.

"I always thought I'd imagined it, that it had all ultimately come from within me," I whisper in a rush. "I don't think I ever allowed that it was, that she, Shama, was…real."

"It *did* come from within you. We humans rarely see things as they truly are," says Lin, "and if we do, our minds invent ways to diminish the experience. To justify to ourselves that the world is merely as we perceive it. We are simply not equipped for a larger reality. Why should we be?"

"Then, why did I see Shama?"

"That is your name for this greater energy; your mind and heart's own picturing of it. You reduce her to a person so that you can perceive her. Such is your skill. Your gift. All we ever see is metaphor. But you see more than most. As does your child."

At that moment, Renshu raises his arms in a welcoming gesture and insists we all stay the night and begin our long journey home to my mother and the other Outdwellers afresh in the morning. Lin turns to Zotzi and I catch Gardner's eye. He nods, and I put an arm around Freya, who is looking pale with weariness.

Eventually, after creating a makeshift bed of cushions and sheets for us on the lounge room floor, and a spot in a spare room for Lin and Zotzi, Meiying and Renshu retire to their room.

Freya falls asleep on the couch between us, her head on my lap, her feet against Gardner. Neither of us makes any move to lift our daughter to her spot on the floor, as though we are holding on to her connecting warmth between us.

We talk about Freya, about her new gift, what it is, how it might work; but we are analytical, a little too polite with one another. Finally, we lapse into silence. On the other end of the couch, he seems so far away.

"We have a long journey home, don't we, Gardner?" I say quietly.

He looks at me. "We do."

I'm about to shift Freya from my lap when he reaches across the top of the couch. Our fingertips meet. I slide my palm beneath his and a familiar flash of yearning spreads throughout my body. I look at our hands and see us clearly for the first time in a long while; each a little older, a little more embattled by the sun, by the bright light of living. And with this seeing comes a great lifting within me; a heavy bird taking flight from my chest.

I stroke Freya's forehead, her sleeping face. We are together. The three of us. And we are well. When I meet his eyes, I find I'm almost smiling.

ACKNOWLEDGMENTS

I'd like to give special thanks to my friends and family who have supported me through this publishing journey. Your encouragement, beta reading and the precious time you've given me caring for my kids, listening to me, all of it; it's been invaluable. So thank you, I truly couldn't do this without you.

Thank you to Leticia for your insightful edits, Paula for your pivotal comments on my early manuscript, and Sue for catching those last page bugs.

Thanks to the wonderful Helen for your supreme editing and to the very patient and talented Shkike (99designs) for your beautiful cover design.

Thanks to Dan, always, and to my wonderful kiddos, Griffin and Kate, for your encouragement and patience with all the tapping from the corner desk.

And to Cinnamon the cat for keeping me company. Hey, wait, that's my keyboard!

ALSO BY ALEXANDRA MANFIELD

The River Daughter (2020)

If you'd like to find out more, please visit:

www.spindlepress.com.au

www.ingramcontent.com/pod-product-compliance
Lightning Source LLC
Chambersburg PA
CBHW020510120726
47904CB00003B/774